TALES FROM THE JESSICA FILES

–

From Bad To Worser

After all, this is a love story in absolute, like time itself.

PUNIS RUSSI

First printing edition 2023.

Published by Secret Freezer Publishing, LLC., PO Box 1025, El Mirage, Arizona, 85335

https://www.secretfreezerpublishing.com
https://punisrussi.me

ISBN: 979-8-9894680-2-7 (Hardcover)
ISBN: 979-8-9894680-3-4 (Paperback)
ISBN: 979-8-9894680-4-1(eBook)

In loving memory of **Shiro Yagami**, a most excellent companion who left us too soon. You will sorely be missed, my friend.

Or Forward?

Punis Russi came to my attention several years ago. Few writers have a daring conversational style and can carry a unique story like PR. He opened my eyes and mind to a world far from commonplace yet convincing in every character and *tête-à-tête*.

This world opens in new and unexpected ways in every colloquy and chapter. The conversations and interactions are delightfully authentic and engaging. Knowing the origins and background makes this even more entertaining.

PR's style is far from cliche and quite unique to his stories or writing. He invites us into a world less seen and rarely experienced, allowing us to share something we would never even consider.

-The Reverend CD for **The Amalgamated Heavy**

Or Contents?

Or Introduction?

Before we begin on this journey, there is something that we here at Secret Freezer Publishing wish to share about the format and structure of these stories.

You see, we view "tales" as a story. The kind of story you'd tell a friend or loved one, sharing and possibly embellishing it.

Our story has no specific timeline; things do happen when they do happen, but this is not a straight line. You'll just have to read all of it for the context, content, and story to come together, like a nice orange chicken sauce.

We hope you can open your mind and read what is written, consume it for its majestic nature, and find the lost corundum... It's out there, on the other side, waiting to be found.

P20 - or BLEEP?

Part 20 twenty of The Jessica Files. This week, we learn how pain rules this loving couple and the lengths they go for one another.

Jessica had already gone to bed that evening without me but with my permission. I had some extra work to finish that night, but something felt off; perhaps it was the intense pain.

I recall that I was in the kitchen, finishing the documentation for The Department of Rules and Contracts, or DORCs for short. Sometimes I feel like dealing with them is worse than dealing with my BLEEP ass knees.

I was about to take my nighttime medication, and then boom, something that would typically happen while I was in bed occurred while I was standing.

An incredibly massive wave of pain washed over my knees, causing me to buckle. I cursed them the first time it happened, saying, "Fuck my BLEEP ass knees, you suck."

The second, third, and fourth times were less kind. The pain swept over me at an ever-increasing rate.

I loudly exclaimed, "Fuck my BLEEP ass knees; you mother fuckers suck."

And shortly after that, Jessica came out to check on me and see what the matter was. She knew it was not good if I was cussing in that regard towards my knees.

But what was exceptionally good was that Jessica was buck-naked, as she would normally be with me when it came time for bed. We always wanted to be close to one another as the amount of energy that our two existences created together was incredible.

I knew that the level of pain that I was feeling meant, well, nothing good. It meant that the deterioration of what was left of the cartilage in my knees was continuing to decay, creating more bone-on-bone friction whenever I moved.

Oh, and the arthritis was picking up at an increasingly worrying rate, another punch in the junk.

I was nearly hunched over when she approached me and put her arm over my shoulder to steady me. I knew that she was fully aware of how much pain I was in. I knew she understood; this wasn't about the guest bed and sleep.

Jessica was more and more concerned about the pain that I was suffering daily. It was getting more debilitating, but not to the point where I would stop doing anything.

Jessica and I knew the stark reality; at the end of the day, I would be in the shower, spraying my knees down multiple times and getting four hours asleep.

It took an ever-increasing toll on my life, but I never took it out on her due to my love for her. And I never took it out on the boys because I love them immensely.

But because I am this guy, I took it out on myself. I always felt like I could be strong enough and had enough strength to continue dealing with it, but I was starting to question my power.

Look, let me be real here. I am physically and mentally strong, but there is only a certain amount of pain that any human can take at any point. And I was exceeding this number on a very regular basis.

I don't know how I was keeping my shit together, but I promise you that Jessica was not the only person who wanted to murder my knees because I wanted to commit a war crime against them.

I turned ever so much towards Jessica, and I could see the smile on her face, that smile I felt like butter being melted smile.

"Thank you, my love; your strength will help me through this because my love for you is so strong."

"Sir, it's getting worse, is it not?"

"Ma'am, it couldn't possibly continue to get worse because it's already horrific as it is, as it were. I am so thankful you're here to give me the additional strength I need to keep going. Without you, where would I be?"

And I goddamn well knew the answer to that question; I wrote a fucking book about it. I'd be lost on the other side and end up in bitter disappointment, having never had my Jessica.

I was never having my one true love, my Ma'am. I would be deprived of that. It would be taken away from me in a fate worse than an eternity at the DMV.

"Jessica, I love you, and there will be no other. I love you so incredibly much, and you know this to be true. I would kill all humans for you, and I would kill all humans with you.

Jessica, you are everything I have ever wanted in a mate. You are absolute, like time itself. I cannot say further how much I love you as it would be sickening."

And then, another wave of pain rocked me, and my buddy shuddered as I stood in the kitchen with Jessica. I knew how bad this was, and so did Jessica. And it's not because she would have to sleep in the guest room without me.

No, it wasn't because I was going to spend an excessive amount of time in the shower, sitting in the tub, and spraying my knees down in hopes that I could appease the Knee Gods to go away and leave me the fuck alone.

"Sir, do you think it's time that we call Dr. Goodknee? You know he will take care of you, and he has in the past. He has done two of your knee surgeries already. Do you think it's time, Sir?"

"No, Ma'am, it's not time yet, but that time is drawing closer. There has to be something we are missing in my diet and light exercise program that is at fault."

"Sir, at the risk of what I'm about to say, and I mean no disrespect—"

I cut her off there. "Ma'am, wouldn't you like to go off the record?"

"Sir, I would like to request off the record, please."

I nodded.

"Sir, don't you think the problem is because you have shit-ass knees?"

"Ma'am, you aren't wrong in your statement, considering the fact that I have little to no cartilage left in my knees."

"Sir, I am incredibly concerned for you, us, and the boys. I can't lose you, Sir." There was a long pause; Jessica seemed unsure of her next steps, as if she was still on the record.

"But, Punis, it's getting worse, and we need to work together to solve this.

"I cannot handle seeing you in pain, and it is incredibly hard not to have you next to me at night. It is a regenerative force to have you with me, Sir, as I know it is for you.

"I love you, Sir. I love you, Punis, and I'm worried because, like, when I pulled you back, I told you, honestly and specifically, you are all I have, and I cannot go on without you."

"Jessica, I understand. My love for you has allowed me to be pulled back by your love. You, and only you, and I have said so openly, honestly, and truthfully, have kept us together.

"Ma'am, without you, who knows where we would be? Jessica, you mean the world to me. You are my life. You are what moves me forward. Without you..." I trailed off, knowing where my brain was going.

Yes, that place. That place where I... I wrote a goddamn book about that place, that fucking Other Side. FUCK!!!

"Jessica, I say this lovingly: Without you in my life, I'd not have made it to this date in time. You know I have expressed as much."

"Punis, please grant me back on the record."

I nodded again.

"Sir, please?"

Oh, how I could never say no to that face, that beautiful smile. That smile. That mother fucking smile. She was so adorable. Plus, she was still naked and not hiding it.

I'll tell you what. The regimen change. Hot damn! She was... my mind went somewhere else.

"Sir, are you here with me?"

There was a bit of a delay on my part.

"Yes, Ma'am, I'm here. You are such a magnificent specimen of a human; you blow my mind away.

"Jessica, if you can give me a sweet and tender kiss, the one you have been known to give me that changes my mind, that sets my mind, that makes me forget who I...":

POW! Right on, my kisser. Jessica planted one on me, which made me understand and get it. Also, she was naked, and I was in pain, the type of sweet and tender kiss, fuck, where was I?

"Jessica, please help me to the shower. And when we get there, please join me and help me steady myself as we spray down my knees. I want you to see what it's like in that place, the one you've never been."

"Sir, are you saying...?"

"Yes, Ma'am, it's time for you to see how bad things are and to give me the strength tomorrow to call Dr. Goodknee to start us going forward."

I paused. Not my usual stupid ass pause; no, this was the pause where the pain...

"Jessica, thank you, my love. Without you..."

Another wave washed over my body, pushing me down to the floor.

"Fuck you, BLEEPS!"

"Sir!"

"Yes, Ma'am, they are BLEEPS! We know this to be true.

"Jessica, let us go to the shower and have you help me. You are ravishing..." I trailed off.

I love this woman so much. So much so that I invited her into yet another world of my life, exposing myself and presenting my vulnerabilities to her on a silver platter. I wasn't worried.

I trusted Jessica with my life, and I know that was reciprocal.

"Jessica, you are so beautiful as a human..." I once again trailed off. "Please help with this once we have gotten past my threshold..." I trailed off yet again.

"Ma'am, I'll fancy you a quickie while we are at it." I winked.

"Sir!"

All I can remember, once we were in the shower, was that Jessica and I were lying in the tub. Her back to my thorax, like the Badness. But this time, she was manning the shower head, spraying my knees and feet down ever so lovingly.

She was just...

"Ma'am, without you..." Yet again, I trailed off, another wave of pain crashing down on me with more and more pain. "Fuck you, Knee Gods, fuck you all! You lousy BLEEPS!"

And with that, Jessica turned to me and requested, "Sir, I need you to take over with the shower wand for a few moments, please."

Jessica handed me the shower wand and rolled over, swinging herself around, going from her back up against my thorax to facing me, sitting across from me with her back towards the water spigot.

And with that, Jessica moved forward to me on all fours; I was the lucky recipient of a loving, tender, and sweet kiss that put me to sleep, lying there in the shower with my one true love.

I think I heard her say, "Sir, I love you. I'll take that shower wand back now, please."

And I swear that was followed up with, "Sir, while I didn't intend for this, it's a good thing I have the shower wand. Very good."

When I came to, some time later, Jessica was lying beside me, both of us still in the tub. The water had stopped running, and the tub was now filled with water for us to lay in.

She had her head on my thorax, arm around my thorax, and Jessica was murmuring something I couldn’t grasp.

"Jessica, how long was I out? The last I recall was that wonderful kiss."

Jessica raised her head off my thorax, winked at me, and said, "Sir, I'm not sure, but I really want a sandwich right now."

P21 - or Repeater?

Part 21 twenty-one of The Jessica Files. This week, we learn how things repeat; This week, we learn how things repeat...

Oh, how Tuesday nights are so exciting in this household. I've written about them and how Jessica and I had to follow etiquette with the contract.

There is so much in our relationship, in any contract relationship, and a large swath of a contract is repetition. You repeat the same tasks over and over and over and with much love.

The contract gave Jessica and me the structure we needed to succeed in a relationship. We had unknowingly craved it for so many years until our orbits gravitated.

When Jessica worked on Tuesdays, I longed for the events always to transpire—a unique set of rules for this evening, as dually agreed to with the DORCs.

"Sir, I'm home!" she'd proclaimed as if I weren't waiting for her in the kitchen, like a kid on Christmas morning. It was always a boost on top of love. It was something extraordinary.

I have always tried to be in my place when I heard the garage go. Jessica would come in, set her stuff down, and come into the kitchen to address me.

When she would come into the kitchen, I could always see that thing we see in someone we love, that we long to be with. Like on Christmas Eve, on Christmas Night.

"Sir? Shall I...?"

I stopped her. "Jessica, please present yourself in front of me. Now."

And there she was, standing before me, beaming from pole to pole, smiling at me. That fucking smile melting me like butter on a summer day here in Phoenix.

"Ma'am, tell me something. Do I love you through and through?"

"Sir, yes, Sir. There could be no doubt. I know this to be true."

"Ma'am, tell me something. Do I love you inside and out?"

"Sir, yes, Sir. There could be no doubt. I know this to be true."

"Ma'am, tell me something. Do you know what either of those means?"

And I heard crickets.

"Ma'am, would you like to know?"

"Sir, please, Sir. I hope that I have not been disrespectful to you. I'd never..."

"Jessica, my love, I do not feel that way. You see, those terms are a play on words. You have an inside and outside collar. Telling you I love you in such a manner shows us that.

And my love of all loves, through and through... well, that's something special. But, you see, that term frequently denotes completion, entirety, an entire state.

Jessica, you are absolute to me, like time itself. You are..."

Jessica smiled. "Sir, are you saying that you love me in such an intense manner?"

"Bitch, you know this to be true."

We both giggled at that; such a dorky statement by this guy. But the truth was, I did love her like that, and she did know it. In return, she loved me so much as to knowingly enter into a contractual relationship and subject herself to The Department of Rules and Contracts, or DORCs for short.

"Ma'am, I love you. Now, let us get back to it."

"But Sir, I have..."

I cut her off. "Jessica, if you want to say something, you need to request off the record; you know this and the process."

Jessica looked me in the eyes and denoted, "Sir, I have to tell you something significant."

I nodded.

"Sir, I hope you know how much I love you, Sir. I will kill all humans for you. I will kill all humans with you. You are the single most important thing in this world. I love you, my Sir. I love you, Punis. I don't need OTR to tell you that."

I blushed. This woman was just so astonishing.

"Ma'am, you are just so lovely. But we have a process to follow. But know this; you are even— "

Jessica strangely cut me off, "Sir, thank you for helping me become the woman who stands before you, who loves you like none other. Thank you for making me whole with the absoluteness of your love."

I felt like I was going to cry; it was so sweet and loving. I just wanted to...

"Jessica..." I trailed off. This wasn't the first, nor the last time this happened as I stared at the most excellent human, my life partner, the one. That one. The only one.

She stood before me and turned away, bowing her head so slightly with her hair pulled up. It was like this every time.

I gently removed her outdoor collar, guiding it around and off of her and into my hands for me to keep safe until she was to leave the house again with my permission.

She said, "Sir, would you put my inside collar on me, please?". And so I did—ahh, contracts, how they do things for all parties involved.

I reached around her neck and thorax and set Jessica's inside collar upon her. I knew she preferred her outdoor collar, given that I made it for her because I loved the fuck out of her.

I gave the woman I loved something of and from me through and through. That was as priceless as the gift, time and again that we all have experienced.

Many thanks to the contract with the DORCs. What will they scheme up next?

I so loved the repetition of the contract and contract life. We knew what to say and do, as if in a play.

Jessica asked, "Sir, may I?".

I replied, "You may."

She slid down her pants; oh boy, she looked fantastic. I could see that the changes in her regimen had really paid off. I'm so glad I've made that adjustment.

Her pants were now down at her ankles; Jessica fixed back on my eyes as she stood before me. It wasn't a showdown; she was waiting on my command.

I smirked and said, "Assume the position, Ma'am." With that command, Jessica was on all fours with her pants down around her ankles, aka the furniture position, while resting on the anti-fatigue pad.

"Sir, I was bad today. I left the house without you, and I accept the punishment that comes with it."

We both damn well knew she left the house for her job, but it's a ritual we live by and many others in the contract world. Also, it's in the contract.

I replied, "How many times were we bad, Ma'am?"

Jessica softly replied, as she always did, with some arbitrary number of spanks she could take without whimpering, even if Jessica knew she'd have difficulty sitting later.

I used to think of her as a trooper, but as the years passed, I knew she was a masochist, which is why we were together, not just on contract but because of absolute love.

Jessica replied, "Once?". I laughed inside at the response, like she was phishing for the correct number. And like always, I gave her a "Go fish..."

"Fine, be it 4."

I laughed out loud, like some sort of maniacal supervillain. If only I were rich. She knew I was playing around this time.

"Jessica, once it will be. I love you, Ma'am".

This was a departure from my usual "plus one" format to whatever she would come up with. But it's not an issue today, no, not today.

And with that, a friendly swift swat on the ass, maybe 20% force. I didn't want to punish her today; no, not today.

"Jessica, please stand up. Now."

"Yes, Sir!" And in a jiffy, she was back in front of me, pants still down.

"Jessica, please pull your pants up. I want you to go to your closet and get changed. Just your underwear and that wife beater we both love."

OK, who am I kidding? That shit was for this guy.

"Sir, I will go get changed. I love you, Sir. You are my first, last, and always. We both know this to be true."

I smiled, and with that, she pulled her pants up and started to head to the bedroom.

"Ahem, Ma'am. Aren't you forgetting something?"

"Yes, Sir, I'm sorry, Sir. Do you want a double, Sir?

I paused, but not my normal pause in the middle of a sentence. Jessica had provided me with fodder for a joke, but I decided against it for some reason. Something was amiss.

"Yes, Ma'am. That would be awfully kind and sweet of you. I love you, Ma'am."

And off Jessica went. I stood there pondering something that was on my mind. It wasn't losing her; it wasn't that not having her feeling. It was...

"Sir, here is your Cromulent Vodka/Zevia. It should be exactly how you like it."

"Ma'am, you bringing it to me is exactly how I like it, how I want it. How lucky am I, Jessica, to have you in my life?"

Jessica smiled, knowing there was no answer she could give me.

"Ma'am, please go get changed as per my original order."

Jessica nodded, and off she went, doing her best not to spill her drink. It was so adorable, it was...

I walked over to the thermostat and made a slight adjustment. It was hot in here, and I didn't want to be sweating when Jessica came back out. Plus...

That is to say, dropping the AC down to 70° is perfectly normal. Well, at least for this guy.

I made my way back into the kitchen, and Jessica came out of the bedroom. Her glass was empty, as was mine.

"Sir, would you like a refill? I would gladly perform that request for you."

"Yes, please, Ma'am."

Jessica went off and was back in a jiffy, drinks in hand. She stopped in front of me, turning to me, squaring up.

"They sure do make a lovely pair, don't they?

Jessica stood there, her head slightly tilted, wondering what the fuck I was talking about. I could see it, feel it. But, oh, fuck, how in love was this guy?

"Jessica, tits cold in here, don't you think? Perhaps a tit nippily?" I giggled like the biggest dork in the world as if seeing incredibly well-configured breasts in a wife beater, when it was cold as hell in the room was something new.

Jessica quickly looked down and then back up, noticing the rather erect nipples she was sporting. Damn, they were incredible before her birthday a few years back. So then, as was her wish, we got them pierced, knowing it would please me.

There was a downside: they were a little less sensitive now, and them being at full attention... I trailed off.

"Sir, let's pound these drinks. Then, when we are done, would you take me to the bedroom and pound me."

She paused. I always believed that was from one of our other experiences.

"Sir, I don't want you to pound me; I misspoke. Would you make love to me?"

And what was off for me dissipated. I could not recall her ever uttering those words in all of the years we've been together. But she said it on her own, and I was so enthralled.

"Ma'am, you are the only human that has earned and deserves that. We are each other's destiny."

P22 - or Bell?

Part 22 twenty-two of The Jessica Files, a #short. Today, we learn why towels are apparently optional in my kitchen.

Jessica! Present yourself.

"Sir, yes, Sir. What can I do for you, Sir?"

Jessica is standing there with a shower cap on her head, having just come out of the shower. She wasn't even wearing a towel. Holy Jebus. I love this woman through and ... hmm, what? What was I saying?

"Sir, are you ok? I mean not to..."

"Jessica... for the love of Zeus, you are jaw-dropping. But, you know, Jessica, fuck, I'm not even going to try."

I giggled, that giggle of seeing a supermodel naked in front of you in real life, and she didn't hide it. But, oh, wait, not all of us have witnessed something so mind-bending before the interwebs.

And I hadn't until Jessica. I might as well write an old-school "Dear Penthouse Forums" letter. Jebus, I'm showing my age some more tonight. Where's my Geritol?

Hmm... what?

"Jessica, get your wet ass bitchass over here, now!" I laughed my way through that.

And then, there she was. She, who is that whom, standing in front of me, in her naked glory for which I could not turn away, wait? How fucking high am I?

"Sir, I'm wet for you right now." And she started laughing hard.

I joined Jessica in that; damn, that's one of those times she brought it strong to the hole; damn, she dunked on that shit.

"Oh Jessica, my Ma'am, my one and only Ma'am. The only Ma'am that I will ever have. How you are the culmination of my existence."

"Thank you, Sir." And in a faux southern accent, "You make me blush like a southern belle."

Yeah, this was the kind of shit that went on before the Collar Ceremony (**P10 ten Collars** of **Tales From The Jessica Files**) many years ago. I could not punish her; I just smiled at her, chuckling at how, once in a while, she had timing.

She's been more subdued since the Collar Ceremony (**P10 ten Collars** of **Tales From The Jessica Files**). I will say one crucial thing: often, she will ask, off the record in lightning fashion, to drop a bomb of a joke.

Classic Jessica.

P23 - or Rock Bottom?

Part 23 twenty-three of The Jessica Files. This week, we get caught up with Sir and Ma'am and the surprises that can happen before contract life.

I called Jessica as I had a few questions for her, and more importantly, I was thinking about her. I wanted to see her, spend time with her, and continue to get to know her. There was no pressure; as far as I knew, it was just two humans who were into one another.

"Jessica, I want to cook dinner for you one night this week. Would that sound good to you?"

"Yes, Sir, that would sound wonderful, Sir."

"Jessica, what do you not eat so I can ensure it's not on the menu?"

"Ass, Sir."

I burst out laughing. Holy shit, that was hysterical.

"I'm sorry, Sir, butt, that's a boundary for me."

"Yes, Ma'am. Taking ass off the menu, what else would you not want me to cook?"

"Sir, I'd like to pass on anything seafood-related at this time. Anything beef, chicken, or pork would be perfect, Sir."

"Are there any specific vegetables that you would like? More importantly, are there any vegetables you would prefer I didn't cook for you?"

"Sir, no asparagus, Brussels sprouts, or kale. Potatoes, broccoli, green beans, I'm a basic gal when it comes to what I eat."

"Basic bitch. Got it. Thank you, Ma'am."

We both chuckled about the statement, knowing it was sarcasm. Classic this guy. "Are there any dietary restrictions like gluten- or dairy-free, vegan, and we'll never talk again..."

This time, I got a chuckle out of Jessica. "No, Sir, all those are fine except the vegans; they taste funny."

I burst out with a belly laugh that was... that was so Jessica. "You crack me up so much. Your timing is often on the mark. You are special, Jessica, you are," and I trailed off.

"Sir, please ensure that whatever we do doesn't lead to someone being gassy. I wouldn't want to deal with that if we had sex after dinner."

I thought I hadn't brought that up, but how do I reply?

"Jessica, that's why we have sex before dinner. That way, you don't have to worry about it."

I could hear her thinking. It was not the kind of statement you would typically get from somebody, especially when discussing cooking dinner.

"Sir, that's an incredible idea, concept. I wonder why people don't think of that more often."

"Jessica, it's because I am brilliant. OK, maybe I'm not brilliant, but I'm at least not dumb or moderately not smart. I think a lot."

Jessica chuckled, knowing that was schtick.

"So, Ma'am, what do you think of me making some oven-roasted chicken, green beans, and your choice between carrots and mini potatoes?"

"Sir, carrots would be fine, Sir. They will be cooked in the oven with the green beans and the chicken, Sir?"

"Yes, ma'am, that's the plan. And I will season them with Special Shit."

"Special Shit?"

"Yes, Ma'am, Special Shit, it's the bomb."

"That sounds wonderful, Sir. What would you like me to bring?"

"Jessica, I want you to bring yourself and be down to fuck." I could hear the start of her laughing pretty hard. "And please know, you'll be working up an appetite, so please ensure you take your vitamins."

Laughing her way through it, she said "Yes, Sir, I will ensure I have extra electrolytes. As you know, Sir, plants crave it."

"Jessica, are you making a joke about...?"

"Yes, Sir, Idiocracy. I love that movie. It's so dumb and funny and dumb."

That was so Jessica, classic her.

"OK, Ma'am, I suggest you pick a night thaaaa..."

And with that, I heard the motion sensors go off that somebody was approaching the front door. And I went to the door to see Jessica. I see... I see. Jessica.

She'd later tell me she'd been on her way to see me when I called her, so she stopped a little up the street as we spoke. I was completely unaware of that, and I can promise you I looked like shit.

"Jessica, please come in. I wasn't anticipating seeing you tonight, and I'm so lucky to..."

And then POW! A kiss that had much feeling to it. It's one that I would get from time to time before our collar ceremony but not very much afterward. The rules are the rules. A new line item is signed, and you own it.

"I err uhh fuck what? How where it what am who? I feel like I sound like Q-Bert."

I paused, a little dumbfounded, "Jessica, I need to order the food as I didn't have it on hand, but again..." Another kiss with emphasis, with passion. But yet it was still sweet and tender and loving, but I sure as shit felt it.

"How about you give me five minutes to order the food from EatterGood, and then I will attend to returning that kiss? Is that amenable?"

"Sir, I'm going to go into the bedroom and get changed. Please come in when you have finished ordering from EatterGood."

As quickly as I possibly could fucking do, I grabbed my phone, opened the app, and ordered the necessary ingredients. Once I had finished, I took a deep breath, pounded my double (4 oz) Cromulent vodka and Zevia, and made my way to the bedroom.

Jessica was waiting for me, seated at the foot of the bed and wearing an adorable blue nighttime outfit.

Wow. I was again lost, not knowing what the fuck was going on.

"Jessica, please stand before me." And then boom, there she was.

"Jessica, you are a remarkable specimen of the human race. And now I'm going to show you how much I believe that."

"Sir, ravish me until..."

And I cut her off. "Bitch, shut the f..."

POW! Another super strong kiss. She was, what? Where am I? Who? Huh?

I pushed her back playfully but did not have a collar to grab because this was pre-P 10. I grabbed her left arm as she landed her butt on the bed she'd previously been sitting on.

I'm... I... I... I... FUCK! She'd made me lose my brain.

"Jessica, stand. I didn't mean to..."

POW! Another kiss rocked me." Who? What? Who? I may be punch-drunk from these kisses. Fuck!

"Sir, are you OK? I didn't mean to do anything to..."

I reached out my right hand to her thorax, knowing that what I would do was innocuous, at best. Loving and silly, for sure. Super silly, for fuck sake.

I lovingly gave her a Rock Bottom, WWF style. When we both hit the bed, we laughed very strongly. As we lay there, I turned to Jessica and said, "Bitch, you are magnificent. I want to be yours, and only yours..." boom, another shot across the bow.

"Jessica, keep this shit up, and you won't get any di..."

P24 - or Trip To Greenland?

Part 24 twenty-four of The Jessica Files, a #short. Tonight, we learn how a night out to see GF could be a hoot.

A little while ago, I mentioned to Jessica that a favorite, Greenland Floyd, the greatest Pink Floyd tribute band in the world, would be performing here in Phoenix, Arizona, and I would like us to go.

"Ma'am, would you like to make a night of it? We could go out to dinner, go to the show, and stay in one of the lovely hotels downtown?"

She was up in front of me as I was finishing the statement. "Sir, that would be wonderful, Sir. Have you decided on any of the details?"

"Well, Ma'am, I was hoping you'd sit with me as I made the decisions for the evening."

I know this is a slight departure from the norm, but I worded it in such a manner to ask for help but also to tell her what I wanted in such a way as she knew.

"Yes, Sir, shall I grab us another round of Cromulent Vodka and Zevia?"

"Ma'am, you are a mind reader. I'd like you to sit with me when you come back."

"Yes, Sir."

And with that, she was off. Although, of course, she didn't make them as I did... the ole slurp'em to move'em schtick. But she was a far better bartender than I'll ever be.

And boom, there she was, drinks in hand. I stared at her most lovingly. I loved this woman through and through. She was everything I could have asked for in a mate. She was infinite.

"Thank you, Ma'am. Please, take a seat here with me."

That was such a fantastic statement, and the feeling that came with it was equally remarkable.

Sitting before my 27-inch display, I brought up the concert hall layout and the available seats. Jessica knew I preferred aisle seats as it reduced my perceived panic attack levels.

"Jessica, my love, what do you think of this section?" Pointing out a spot that was least problematic for me. She knew that this would be painful for me, not just physically.

"Sir, you love me so much as to seat us there?" She peered over her shoulder at me, knowing I did.

"Bitch, you know this to be true!"

We both laughed hard, and Jessica leaned back onto my thorax. Hmm, this was new.

"Jessica, I love you. There could be no doubt."

"Yes, Sir. And I love you irregardlessly."

"Jessica, I will book us those seats. What do you think of going for some nice steaks at the Magical Meat Magician?".

"Sir. You really do love me."

Jebus, this, too, was new. She was gleeful of my plans. It had been some time since we went out, and I was still recovering from The Great Panic Attack.

We'd also not been away from the boys, Shibby and Tibor, since losing Fluffle. I did not want to bring any of that up, knowing it would just upset me, and I didn't want to deal with my emotions blowing up that spot.

"Jessica, the last part will be a hotel for the night. We've stayed at many of them over the years, and I'd like your thoughts on which you think I would prefer. The ZZZed Hotel & Resort or The Clankers Hotel?"

Nearly instantly, Jessica responded, "Sir, there could be no doubt. The Clankers Hotel."

I smiled at Jessica; she was such a remarkable specimen of a human. And I loved the fuck out of her.

"Ma'am, I'll take care of booking all of this if, and only if, you can do the following things for me.

- Give me a sweet and tender kiss,
- Make us another round, and
- Get changed into a lovely nighttime outfit that..."

POW! Right on the kisser. This kiss had some extra oomph to it. And that spoke to me. LOUDLY.

Jessica got up from where we were seated, grabbed our empty glasses, and made her way to the kitchen. I was unaware of where she was going with this, but I was game to see the results.

A few seconds after I had wrapped up all the plans, Jessica walked out of the kitchen, buck naked, carrying two Cromulent Vodka/Zevia. My jaw must have hit the floor. Twice.

"Holy hell! Jessica... Mind... Functioning... Blown... Who?"

"Thank you, Sir. I appreciate the regimen change and the effects that it has had on my mind, body, and soul. I owe this all to you, Sir."

I mumbled incoherently.

"Sir, would you like to..."

I looked her in the eyes sternly and cut her off.

"Ma'am, how dare you!" I giggled as I finished that sentence.

I grabbed the ring on her collar rather firmly, more so than normal. I slowly pulled her into me; all the while, she was holding the drinks in her hands. I was trying to do this without making a mess of the drinks.

As I guided her to me, we stared into one another's eyes. I was doing this to make a point, but also, I love the fuck out of this woman.

I brought her nose to nose with me, and all the while, she balanced the drinks in her hands. This was a test.

"Ma'am, fancy yourself a quickie?"

Her eyes lit up like a Festivus pole. But she did not move, and she did not spill either drink. She just was bent over in front of me, the naked love of my life.

"Jessica, I want you to prove your love for me. Can you do that?"

"Sir, yes, Sir."

"Ma'am, do you think you could handle me touching you in a very loving way without spilling either of those drinks?"

There was a pronounced pause. I long felt she was weighing her odds.

I waited a few seconds, unsure of why she hadn't replied.

"Jessica, I did ask you a question, and you have not replied to me. I'd very much like to hear from you."

"Sir, I mean no disrespect. I...I...I," and she trailed off. This was new...

"Jessica, I love you. Please set the drinks down and kneel in front of me. Now."

And in a jiffy, there she was. I reached down and grabbed the ring on her collar, but this time, I pulled on it harder than I recall. Not to harm or hurt but for a purpose.

"Ma'am, you are ravishing. And I'm going to ravish the shit out of you tonight until you can no longer be ravished. And this won't be quick. But I promise that you will love it, and so will I.

"I love you, Jessica, and I know you love me. I do not want to harm you, but I mean to..."

POW! Right on, my kisser. Stronger than I can recall her initiating in some time. I stood up, put my hand out, and she put her hand into mine.

I gave her a little head nod towards the bedroom, and we walked there together, hand in hand. As we reached the doorway, I gently tugged her hand to stop.

"Ma'am, I came back from The Other Side for you, to be with you. I love you. And now I'm going to show you just how much love that is."

I grinned. Oh, how this guy was going to have a lot of fun with his gal tonight.

P25 - or Shopping?

Part 25 twenty-five of The Jessica Files. This week, we learn how a cover comes to pass, and the music brings this couple back together.

It was a lovely day in early fall here in Phoenix; it was only 95 degrees out, but it was still early. We loved the time of year when it was under 100*, but closer to 50 degrees since we loved having the bedroom windows open at night, throwing blankets on the bed, a couple of cats, and cuddling.

"Jessica, please present yourself in front of me. Now."

And, like always, in a jiffy, there she was. The love of all of my love that I have ever loved that anyone has ever loved. Ok, I'll stop.

"Jessica, I have a fun day planned for us, and I believe you will most certainly enjoy it."

"Sir, please be here to share that with me."

"Ma'am, we will play fashion runway until we have gone through all the clothes in your closet, separating what I want to keep and what we will donate to Goodwill."

"Yes, Sir, we do this yearly, and I enjoy it immensely."

There was a pause. "Sir, I mean no disrespect, but as it's still early, and the ritual indicates drinks, is it appropriate to have a drink while we do this?"

"Yes, Ma'am, let's have some mimosas to make this more fun."

"Yes, Sir, right away, Sir."

Off she went to prep the drinks. I took a chair from the kitchen table and moved it into the usual spot for this ritual of ours. I enjoyed it thoroughly.

And then, there she was with drinks in hand. She handed me one; I smiled that smile at her, the one where she knew I was the one, her one, that one. No, no, no, no!

"Ma'am, would you like to propose a toast?"

"Sir, here is to the eve of the day which will never come, and Sir here is to retreat to ease the pain."

"Ma'am, I love you. You know this to be true."

We clanked, took a swig (gulp), and then I pointed to where I wanted Jessica to go. And the fact that I have to type this, no, it wasn't towards my junk.

"Ma'am, here are my rules for fashion runway show-off time. My role in this will be to instruct you on what we will keep vs. what we will donate. I will grant you the discretion of what you'd like to present to me. You can only present any item, aside from shoes, once."

I chuckled to myself that I'd likely not know she had shown me something twice, having frequently been mentally absent with her walking away from me.

"Jessica, I am entrusting you to find the best outfits to determine the outcome. Please, do not disappoint me."

"Sir, yes, Sir."

And off she went. I watched her walk away, but this time, all I could do was stare at her ass. It looked amazing—the regimen for the win.

I realized I had finished my drink, so I made my way into the kitchen, made another mimosa, and returned to my chair just in time for, well, you know what will happen here.

Jessica comes out in that goddamn hippy skirt outfit. My jaw dropped. "Bitch, how dare you! Burn that fucking outfit, please!"

We both giggled hard. She walked over, bent forward to me, and planted a sweet and tender kiss on me. It was phenomenal.

"Ma'am, that was a wonderful, wonderful kiss. But I still want to burn that fucking outfit. I don't want to give it to Goodwill, for someone there would..." I trailed off, playfully annoyed.

"Sir, I will put it in the donate pile. I wore it for another kiss I wanted."

"How devilish of you, Ma'am. I both appreciate and dislike it at the same time. I will give you an OTR pass for that. But, be warned, I will not be as kind the..."

Boom. Jessica planted another one on my kisser. I may have been punch-drunk; she was bringing it strong.

"Jessica, please continue your task."

And with that, Jessica stepped out of the outfit directly in front of me and walked to the bedroom, tossing the clothing haphazardly to indicate she did it for fun. She was being spicy.

Hmm, next round, Bloody Marys? Now that sounds most excellent.

Jessica comes out with the next outfit: a lovely pair of jeans with rips in the lower thigh area and a stylish white/red Converse t-shirt.

"Ma'am, they stay. No discussion. I love that outfit, especially on you."

Jessica smiled, that pretty smile she had.

"Ma'am, what a great choice to make up for that fucking hippy skirt. FUCK! Ok, Jessica, please proceed to the next outfit."

"Sir, yes, thank you, Sir."

After a short while, Jessica came again. She is wearing what I'd only consider a golf outfit this time. Except we don't go golfing.

I loved the years of playing golf before Jessica, but the knees and the surgeries some years back, before Jessica, and made it not something that was going to happen.

"Ma'am, I think that should go in the donate pile."

"Sir, yes, an excellent choice, Sir."

"Jessica, take your time on this one. You are currently one for three. Not exactly the kind of odds I'd want in anything other than baseball."

Jessica smiled at me. It was an odd smile that appeared to have pressure riding on it.

I made another mimosa, knowing Jessica would be a little longer as she tried to find something to even the score. She was a smart cookie.

Just as I sat down, Jessica came out wearing a little black dress, but it was adorable, cute, and sexy as all fuck. It was her; it was a pillar moment in our relationship.

"Jessica, my love of all loves. I need you to do something for me. I have an idea, but I need you to be... Just stay put, don't move. I have an idea."

I nearly ran out of the room towards my office, sliding along the floor like Tom Cruise. Once in, I grabbed my Hi-Def camera, lenses, and tripod and made a beeline back to the kitchen, back to Jessica.

Once I arrived back in the kitchen, I told Jessica, "Ma'am, I have a special treat today. I want you to help me set up the rig here. I want to take your picture. I think you and that outfit would make for an exceptional cover."

"Cover, Sir?"

"Yes, my love. I believe a silhouette of you in that outfit would be mind-breaking, perhaps so hypnotic as to stop traffic."

"Sir, I mean no..."

"Jessica, that combination on this day at this time, you are far... You are transcendent. You are far more than extraordinary. You eclipse that.

"Right now, Jessica, at this moment, not only are you astonishing to me, but you have given me an idea for something so unique, so unique, so fitting, so my Jessica.

"Ma'am, you are eternal. I can't find enough superlatives. You are just so fucking super fucking hot."

"Sir, thank you. Sir. That is so kind and loving..." And with that, Jessica blushed like I don't believe I've ever seen her do so.

I.. I... I was blown away. I always knew she was the most beautiful human on the planet, the most attractive human on earth, the sexiest. You get the point.

"Jessica, I want your picture so I can keep you frozen in this moment. I want to be frozen in this moment. I feel like we might need to put on some of LSE's (Low Self Esteem - The band's) music."

"Sir, please? Can we, Sir? That would be so us. Please?"

Oh fuck, who was I to refuse?

"Ma'am. How about this? Why don't you make us some of your fan-fucking-tastic Bloody Marys, and while you do that, I will put some LSE on? Is there something you'd like, or just Memorable?"

"Sir, please, Sir. Put on Memorable from Frozen in Fargo. You know that is my absolute favorite LSE song. It reminds me of us, perhaps..."

And she trailed off. This was very unusual; I can't recall the last time this happened. I know I wanted to say something, but also, I wanted her to be there at that moment.

"Sir, I'm sorry. I know how important Sapphire is to you; Memorable is my Sapphire. I..."

"Ma'am, please come here. I want to hug you."

And in a jiffy, she was right in front of me.

"Ma'am, please hug me. I want you lovingly close to me. I've never wanted to be just Memorable to you, nor did I want you to be a Sapphire."

"They really do embiggen us, don't they, Ma'am?"

Oh, how was that not a nerd shot?

"Sir, is that why we drink Cromulent Vodka?"

I pushed Jessica back a shade, grabbed the ring on her collar, and gently pulled her towards me, nose to nose. This felt much more intimate, but I can not tell you why. It was so...

"Jessica..."

"Sir?"

"I waited a lifetime to meet you, I waited a lifetime to hold you, and I waited a lifetime for you to be mine.

"Above and beyond anything else I can say, I can only tell you what my father told me for as long as I can remember. It was such an endearing statement. It is why I have said it to you many times. You are so much. I love you, **Jess**, I love you."

And there was that. It was the first time since the day of our collar ceremony, however many years ago. This could be a sin, but...

"Sir? It's been ages since you called me that. Years and years, Sir. Holy shit!"

"Ma'am, please forgive my statement and for using the wrong namespace. I accept whatever punishment you see fit."

"Sir, I believe we were off the record, weren't we?"

She did something I had done so many times; she cast shade on me, knowing I had fucked up but unwilling to penalize me, knowing damn well I would punish myself for it.

"Thank you, Ma'am. I'm not sure what came over me. I mean no disrespect, on or off the record. I mean, no disrespect if I didn't recall that we were OTR. I'm sorry, Jessica. I know how you feel about that name; it is how I feel about Dude. I hope you find it in your heart to forgive me."

"Sir, can I finish those Bloody Marys and return to showing off to you?"

"Yes, Ma'am. But, Ma'am, can we ensure we are on the record?"

"Sir, we are on the record."

I smiled at Jessica.

"Ma'am, I love you. How about you come here, give me a sweet and tender kiss, and then get back to it?"

And with that, after an inspiring kiss, she returned to the drinks. It allowed me to start working on the lighting for the shot.

It was a "Once in a Live Time" opportunity. I was so excited that I was able to get myself into the moment. Fuck, I need to do that.

I made my way to the audio setup, some old-school Polk cabinets with an equally old-school Marantz head unit, just like my family had when I was growing up.

I queued up some LSE, first with Memorable and then with Sapphire. I added a few others, Breaking Down, Shuckers, Released, and Overhead Lights to the queue, unaware of what would come to pass.

Like a ninja, Jessica was waiting for me with one of her most excellent Bloody Marys. Always delectable. The thing, though, while I'd watched her make them a million, billion, trillion times, if not once, I couldn't tell you her magic. She used non-fish-based ingredients, yet she made the best Bloody Marys in Phoenix, bar none.

I took a sip. Fuck, that was delicious and spicy, but not stupidly so. Not too much horseradish, but a wide pallet that was fan-fucking-tastic.

"Ma'am, I don't know how you do it. You are a magician, sorcerous, just gifted. You are everything."

"Thank you, Sir. My father, rest his soul, taught me how to make them for him when I was a kid. I suppose this is why I like vodka as much as I do."

Oh shit, had I fucking spun us out here, too! Damn it, Punis!

"Ma'am, I think there is something we need to get back to, agreed?"

"Yes, Sir, on it, Sir."

As Jessica walked past me, I gently grabbed her arm, slowly spinning her back toward me. When she arrived, I gently (I know, I know) grabbed her hair from behind, then held the ring on the front of her collar.

I brought her before me, nose to nose, holding her in place as if in stasis. I think this was the only time this had happened in all our years together.

"Ma'am. You did not kiss me as you passed "Go". Therefore, you do not collect $200." I snickered.

Jessica giggled and nodded slightly, given how I was holding her.

"Ok, Ma'am, let's get to this shoot; I believe this will be so mind-blowing that we'll..." And the music starts. I know better than to keep going; this was her time.

I continued to set up the shot, enjoying the fuck out of LSE. Then, like a bolt of lightning, it hit me. How could I have been so blind as not to see this? Or hear it.

Holy hell. I paused the song, much to my dismay of Jessica. She turned to me with a look that said, "Dude, what the fuck?" but without saying it.

"Ma'am, when I had the great panic attack, I...I...I told you that I heard music, but I could not tell what it was, who it was, but I knew it was something we'd listened to together."

"Yes, Sir, I've long wondered what you heard."

"Ma'am, this song and your love brought me back."

I paused, not that pause, but I wanted to see what Jessica did or said.

She got up from the chair I had been sitting in, walked over to me, and outstretched her arms to me, similar to Christmas Eve day so many years ago and Christmas night the following night.

She hugged me, pulling herself in tight and close. I stood there with her, holding her with much love.

"Sir, I love you more."

It was so wonderful that I remembered something from that incredibly traumatic experience for both of us. But, of course, there was a downside to my noting this to Jessica; she was upset, tears rolling down her cheeks, but they were tears of happiness, and I knew exactly why. This would be the fourth time I had seen her cry in all our years together.

"Ma'am, can you assist me in finishing the setup here so we can do these pictures? As I said earlier, I have a wonderful idea for them, and I believe it will make for the most amazing cover that anyone will ever see."

"Sir, I still don't understand. Would you be so kind as to tell me what you're thinking?"

This was a little odd, given that this was a question that Jessica would ask off the record, but we were back on the record thanks to her ingenuity and intelligence to ensure that we were covered.

"Jessica, I want to use the picture I have in mind for the cover of my most recent book, Pain Boomerang, but in a silhouette to protect your privacy. I believe it will make for an incredibly moving image that captivates people's minds. They will wonder who you are, like I did on the other side."

"Sir, that is incredible. I am incredibly honored to be allowed to be your cover girl. It is so touching for you to think of me that way."

"Ma'am, from the first time I saw you at the store so many years ago, I...I...I need to get this moving; we still have lots of outfits to go through. And if we are lucky, there could be some us time.

Ma'am, before we start some fun picture time, I want you to know that I had hoped we would be able to clean out the closet a little and then go shopping to get you something to wear to dinner tonight."

"Dinner tonight?"

"Yes, Ma'am, your friend eXXa wants to introduce us to her new partner."

Jessica looked at me in scorn. Not for me, but because she did not like eXXa. I'd long thought she felt competitive with her, but I never understood why.

Jessica was far, FAR more intelligent. Jessica was far, FAR more attractive, better built, sexier, hotter, everything-er. Jessica had developed into a truly complete package.

However, I dare not ask about this rivalry without granting a lengthy OTR session that was an expletive-laced epitaph of a tirade, like watching curling.

At this moment, I understood why she'd bring up things about hooking up with eXXa, presenting herself -it would appear- as disappointed that we didn't. Yet, she was happy underneath that odd facade, knowing it would never happen.

And let's be clear here: I wanted one woman, and only the one, my Jessica. None other. I do not share, no matter how much I thought a three-way with Jessica, Lexie Blue, and Foxy Monroe would be mind-blowing to watch.

No, she was mine as I was hers. No one else, I meant it. She meant it. The DORCs meant it.

"Sir. Do we have to? Do we have to go to dinner with her? I think I feel a case of Anthrax-Creeping Death-The Plague coming on."

I straight up busted out laughing. How fucking smart was she? That was so Jessica. She was endless.

P26 - or Flirting?

Part 26 twenty-six of The Jessica Files, a #short. This week, we learn a little more about our favorite couple's flirtatious pre-story.

These events happened sometime before Christmas Eve day. While I can not specifically note the dates and times of these interactions, they most certainly happened.

I am telling these as slightly edited (spelling, grammar) conversations with Dana. It's important for the context of all the things that happened beforehand and to show why Dana is so important to this story. Without her... and I trailed off.

This is what started it all—the **Hello Hello** game. I never imagined that this one little thing would lead to the beautiful life that Jessica and I have today.

As best I can recall, our first interaction was when I checked out at the register, and Jessica was doing the bagging. We had seen one another a few times, casually checking out the score.

I mentioned to the rather distracted cashier that I'd like to grab a bag of the ridiculously strong-smelling cinnamon-scented bags of pinecones.

Jessica jumps into action and states, "I'll get you one, sir." She returned shortly thereafter and told me, "If it's not cinnamony enough for you, just swap it out on your way out."

I just stared at this very attractive woman. I never would have imagined this is where things would go, not in a million, billion, trillion years.

"Thank you, ma'am."

And then, business began to pick up.

The phone rang, and the cashier picked up the phone and said, "Hello?" so I said, "Hello?" and then Jessica said, "Hello?" To the two of us. I turned to Jessica and said, "Hello?" to which she replied, "Hello?". Not willing to leave it there, I said, "Hello?" to which Jessica replied, "Hello?" back to me."

It was ridiculous. When I got to the car, I texted Dana to tell her about this unique exchange.

After some chuckling, Dana commented to me, "That was super adorable. You became a real person to her." And I think she was right.

Another instance of this was what has been called the Basket Pipe Bomb. I had checked out and was making my way to the exit, and Jessica was standing there talking with one of the managers with whom I had become familiar.

And Jessica was not facing me, so as I walked towards her and passed her, I took my hand basket and dropped it into the shopping cart she was holding.

And I turned around, spinning back to her if you will, and I got that scolding face, that scolding look from Jessica and the finger point. And she mouths to me, "You!" Classic Jessica.

One afternoon, right before Thanksgiving, I was shopping in the store. I was on my way over to the cheese section as I was trying to find the fucking eggs that seemed to have been hidden like on Easter. Frustrated, to say the least.

Jessica walked past me with a handcart in tow and commented, "You're back!"

I was a little stunned, not expecting to see her, let alone hear from her. I paused and noted, "I'm here as much as you are."

In some weird universe thing, we both chuckled at the statements we had made.

I found the eggs and was headed towards the frozen section to find my muffins when Jessica walked by and stated to me, "...except I'm the one getting a tiny little paycheck."

I turned back to look at her, stunned once again by her beauty. And I said, "We both do realize that my shopping here in some small part pays your said tiny little paycheck, right?"

Jessica smiled. That smile, that fucking smile.

After checking out, I got to the car and texted Dana to tell her of this latest interaction. We had a good laugh over my being such a dork.

Another flirtatious move this guy made happened one evening. This was after the time that Jessica would later tell me was when she fell in love with me, **P17 seventeen - Tear**.

At first, Jessica was bagging in the line I was in, and as I had just finished putting my items on the conveyor belt, I looked up to see her walking to another checkout lane.

I casually said, "Yo..." and that got her attention. She said, "You'll be fine," and then chuckled.

I was annoyed by this in a very playful way. So, I needed to up the ante and knew just how. I started talking to her over two registers and a handful of people. It was pretty silly, all things being equal.

In a loud enough voice that she heard me but wasn't yelling, I matter-of-factly told her, "Hey, you should come back. I shop here because of you."

Afterward, I shared this interaction with Dana when I got to the car. She was rather amused by it, knowing how much of a dope I was. She coined #**ISHBU** (I shop here because of you). It was just so god damn funny, and I was in stitches.

P27 - or Pre-starter?

Part 27 twenty-seven of The Jessica Files. This week, we learn how some things happen outside... oh, fuck, just read...

These are the events that happened before Po zero of the Jessica Files. It's not something that Jessica likes me to talk about, but in this particular case, I thought it was fascinating and essential to share with everybody because it happens to all of us.

When Jessica and I went to Hello Shen Go on our first date, Christmas night, so many years ago, a bit more happened than previously reported; Jessica was near freak-out and almost panic attack level. As we sat at the table and talked, she continued to get paler by the moment, and I could tell that something was off.

"Jessica, are you OK? You look pale. Is there something I can do for you?"

"Sir, I...I...I don't feel good right now and am starting to freak out."

"Jessica, what's the matter? Please tell me; I'm interested."

"Sir, I think I'm going to have a panic attack, and..." she trailed off.

I took a second to scan the room to see if I could discern anything that would be a trigger, and I saw two friendly police officers. Hmm, I don't recall seeing them when I walked in.

That couldn't be the reason, now could it? Her father was in law enforcement; she'd grown up around that life. The plot thickens like a nice orange chicken sauce.

"Jessica, please tell me what's happening, and I will help you."

"I'm sorry, Sir, I am having a problem right now and... Can you excuse me so I can go to the ladies' room and regroup?"

I looked at her directly and said, "Jessica, get your shit together. I can't exist in this reality without you here with me."

I discovered the issue many years later, but I have always tried to be respectful and helpful without being an overbearing parent.

"Jessica, go freshen up and take a couple of deep breaths. Then, when you come back, you can tell me what's the matter. Is that fair?"

"Yes, Sir, I will do my best."

She got up and walked to the restrooms, and as she walked away, I wondered if I would see her again. I had that "staring at her ass walking away" feeling as I was unsure if she would return. I mean, by fucking, for real.

As time ticked on, the waiter brought our drinks, which happened to be the same thing—a double Vodka Ginger ale with a slice of lime.

I drank mine, nearly in a full shot. And I waited a couple of minutes, and then I drank Jessica's. I'm not going to let her drink get all watered down and go to waste, right?

And then, things started to get more interesting. While sitting there, one of the police officers stopped by on their way to the restrooms and asked me a very poignant question.

"Is everything OK, sir?"

"Yes, Officer. Jitters..."

"She was looking peaked, and I didn't know if anybody needed help, so I wanted to stop and check if everything was OK."

"Thank you, officer; that is very kind of you and is a value I hope many more people have in this world. But it's our first date, and she's having a bit of a panic problem, so I suggested she go to the restrooms and recollect herself."

I continued, "I hope she didn't walk out the back door because that would be horrifying for a human to experience when working on starting a new relationship."

"Well, sir, I hope everything works out, and I didn't mean to be a bother."

"Officer, I will reiterate what I said before. It is very kind of you and is a value that I hope many more people have in this world."

And with that, the officer turned and walked away, heading to the Men's room. At this point, I was starting to wonder if Jessica had left or not, and I was beginning to have a little bit of a panic attack myself.

A female wait staff member walked by, and I stopped her. "Miss, I need a favor, and I would greatly appreciate it if you could help me out."

She stopped and looked at me, then turned to square up and said, "Yes, sir, what can I do for you?"

"Well, my date, she was not doing well, and she went into the restroom to gather herself. I'm just concerned about what has happened to her, as it's been about 20 minutes. I don't know if she walked out, and I don't know if she's in the bathroom having a panic attack and crying uncontrollably.

"Could you go into the women's restroom and ask if she is there? Her name is Jessica, and if there's no response, I know this will be a big ask, but can you check not under each stall but in each stall to see if she's there? I would be very grateful."

She smiled at me and said, "Sir, I understand, and I will take care of that for you."

I smiled at her and knew this would cost me some money because it was a big ask with extensive requirements. And I'm not above giving somebody a little bit of cash as a thank you.

A couple of minutes later, the gal came out of the Ladies' restroom, walked back over to me, sat at the table with me, and began explaining what was happening.

"Jessica is in the bathroom and is incredibly nervous. And took some medication to try to deal with that beforehand, but it has made her a bit more panicky."

Well, at least she hasn't left yet. LOL

"I might have a solution or some remedy, but I can't ask you to do something, and I can't go into the lady's bathroom. I mean, right?"

She commented, "So long as there's nobody else in the restroom, and in this situation, I will ensure you are covered."

"Thank you, and I greatly appreciate it and to show my appreciation. I have something here for you." I take a fifty-dollar bill out of my pocket and gently and kindly slide it to her across the table.

I continued, "Good people in this world show kindness. Soon, you'll have to ask for that from someone. I know how much it means to others when you do that."

And with that, she took the fifty-dollar bill and returned to her tasks. I stood up, waved to my waiter, and he came over. "I am not leaving but must go into the lady's room to get my date." I rolled my eyes and said, "Yeah, that's where I'm at."

As I walked to the ladies bathroom, I noted that I really should put something bigger than a fifty in my wallet. I knocked on the door and dorkily asked, "Is there anybody in here whose name isn't Jessica who is on a date with me?" Crickets.

"Jessica, I'm coming in..." I chuckled; oh, how that could make for a perfect sex joke, but it would probably be disappointing... just like sex... With me. Damn, rare form tonight.

I walk in; "Jessica, what stall are you in?". And she shyly indicates the first one. I walk over and open the stall up, hoping she's not going to the bathroom; again, it's a perfect joke there. Unfortunately, she's still a little pale, sweaty, and clammy, and I have to find a way to solve this. And I did, kind of.

"Jessica, if this is a test for me, I will blow it up. If this is a test for you, I will not allow you to fail. I have panic attack problems, and sometimes, they're downright scary. So, I always keep a particular medication with me as it helps calm my nerves."

You'd think I'd be talking about cocaine; that's a different story.

Jessica, if you take my hand, things will get better, and you have to believe and have faith in me in a blind faith way. I can make things less worse, but you have to put your hand out and take what is in mine."

And like what would come to pass a million, billion, trillion times, if not once in our relationship, her hand was out seemingly before I finished the sentence.

I put my hand on top of hers and let go of myself so I could grab hold of her and bring her back to where we were.

I knew there was more to this than what I had been told, and I knew that I would get the rest of the information from Jessica, but not right and there as I was not going to interrogate her.

We left the ladies' room and made our way back to our table, hand in hand. God damn, she has so much potential. If only I could harness that.

Our waiter came over and asked if we wanted another round. "Yes, please, I'll take a double, and she can have whatever she desires."

"I'll have the same, but standard. Thank you, Sir."

She turned and looked at me across the table, that look I would get from Jessica; it was so her.

"Jessica, since you will be with me for the rest of our natural lives, I must disclose that I suffer from panic attacks, which can sometimes be horrific. I felt like I would have one yesterday, Christmas Eve Day when you came over to hug me.

"I do not take this situation with you lightly and do not need an explanation right now, but I want you to know that compassion and love come in various flavors—" And she cut me off."

Sir, thank you. I understand now the kindness and compassion you are showing me. And I appreciate the latitude that you have afforded me tonight.

"Please know this is not typical, and I mean no disrespect. I can only hope to spend the rest of my time in this life or the next with you."

As we sat across the table, I said to Jessica, "Why don't you come over and sit next to me?"

And in a jiffy, she was sitting next to me, on my left, where she would be seated for the rest of our lives. I always wanted her next to me, and after however many years on we are and after however many contracts we've signed, I've always wanted her there, next to me.

"Jessica, I am so thankful you stayed and didn't leave me because I wouldn't want to live in a world where you walked away from me, and I did not stop you. It would be so disheartening and painful that..." I trailed off.

"Sir, I never want to leave you, and I never want to be without you. I'm sorry my emotions got the better of me and..." She trailed off, too.

The waiter returns with our drinks, and I turn to Jessica and raise my glass. "I have a toast; this is the toast I use when I toast. Since we didn't toast our first drink, we will toast this one because this is new.

Here's to the eve of the day which will never come. And here is to retreat to ease the pain."

I offered my glass out for a clank, and we clanked. I just knew, I just knew that getting over this hump would make us whole. This was a new beginning.

P28 - or All The Light?

Part 28 twenty-eight of The Jessica Files. This week, we get a guest post by the great K.W. Turner, a #short. Such a treat!

Thank you to K.W. Turner for this most unexpected contribution. Without you, our lives would be incomplete. Thank you for being a Super Villain with me—just as the lifelong homies we will always be.

K.W. and I talked one day after the launch of our most recent books. The topic was a continued collaboration between us. I had an idea, one that I'd have told him about during our sessions.

> Yes, the sessions. I will quote from K.W.'s most wonderful book, **The Other Side, Chapter 0:**

These writings are a story from a friend whom I hadn't spoken to in some time. I believe that they were lost in their mind, struggling. This is my translation of the story they presented to me and ghostwritten by myself with permission.

Yup, That's about the two of us and that journey. It was like going to see your therapist (if you were to have one), and things just came out because you were in a warm, safe, and loving place.

I'd be remiss not to state this first and foremost... To my friends and family, good lord, they didn't want to hear it. It was too much for them, unwilling or unable to help.

It didn't matter the level of torment someone was suffering for so long, causing so much pain. You know, the one where you had the fear of having to deal with the whole thing that you'd rather ignore.

We've all been there, one way or another. But I digress.

The events of this short take place sometime before **Chapter 12, Disillusion** of **The Other Side** by **K.W. Turner**.

This wasn't the first, but it would be one of the last mornings when I awoke in a panic, sweating profusely and totally freaking the fuck out.

I recall waking from a slumber and seeing her, the girl from the grocery store. She was there, seemingly more than she should be. Yet, another night and another dream with her in it.

However, this was radically different. No, this was the antithesis of normality. It was her, but instead of being close to me, like the hug of all hugs from Christmas Eve Day so many years ago, she was drifting away from me.

I could see her frantically fighting it. In those times, in my mind, she was alive and a part of me.

I just... I... had to live with my inactions and their consequences—a real skull-crusher. I had to live with my own shit. I'm pretty good at that. It's a virtue.

I didn't know what I could do to catch her as she dissipated in my mind's eye. So surreal. It was only one of two or three instances where something like this had happened.

I thought to myself, "Dude, for fuck's sake, wake the fuck up. HEY!! Wake the fuck up, dumb ass!

"This isn't the goddamn alarm clock. You can't sleep through this one. This is your reality checking-in. She. Doesn't. Exist. Anymore.

"Dude! All of us, all of the "Puniverse that we know of," want her to be real again. Hell, even "heart" wants that shit to be really real.

"And you know that mother fucker is made of coal."

My goodness, my internal space was conspiring against me, or at least picking on me for being such a dumb ass. They are my enemy inside. Those fucks!

This went on for years, a part of the pummeling of my soul and the torture caused to my mind. I drank to make those cunts stop ruining everything. Everything. Yes, everything.

And still, it went on, day after day after day after day. I might as well be telling the story of Cavern on The Green from Futurama, S06E07 -The Late Philip J Fry. Classic.

I have to lighten the mood sometimes, knowing how close I am, well, "we" are, to losing it. One something too many that break us breaks me—something crushing the coal into something far more shiny.

Thinking about her, the girl from the grocery store, that day may as well be the only time I think I've been happy as an adult. She was something else, my STNR. Damn, I need a better name for her.

Each time that dream happened, it was predicated by more emotional slaps to the junk with a Wiffle Ball Bat. And then the panic attacks would come.

And in those times when I could exist there with her, it was wonderful. I could feel like we had such a marvelous life together. Something worthy of narration.

But that isn't the reality in which "we" live. Nah, I might as well refer to it as existing. Holding on by a thread, knowing all the while that the littlest thing, or things, could push us over the edge into... into...

Well fuck, now that I'm up, awake, and angry again, I might as well take a stroll to the park to see if that would help clear my mind and attempt to rid myself of so much pain...

It's just beneath the surface. Slowly but steadily ripping my being into pieces, finally consuming me. I have nowhere to run, hide, or ask for help.

And yet, I could... I could go to the park, maybe find and snag a bench, and enjoy myself and the world if not for a spell. Now, that would be lovely.

P29 - or The Outcome?

Part 29, twenty-nine of The Jessica Files, a #short. This week, we learn how crazy Punis is.

The outcome... I fear that it is something that I can see, and it is so close that I can grab ahold of it. But when I reach out, I realize it is much too far away, and I can't possibly bridge that gap.

Several years ago, I was in a very different spot before meeting Jessica. I was looking at two knee surgeries in less than two months. I knew I would put my life on hold, which was scary.

Even though I had been in and out of relationships for some time, I always knew it was because of me and not the other party, but I also knew that pain played a considerable role in my existence. Not just because I'm a Dom, but because I have shit-ass knees.

I was always hopeful that I would find somebody who fulfilled me and allowed me to take a deep breath, take a step back, open my arms, and accept them into my life. I am not talking about religion, fuck those BLEEPS.

I was fighting an inner conflict between my personality facets and the reality I lived in. I always felt like I could never win, which is why I denote that frequently. But at that time, it felt like I had something within my grasp, only to watch it slowly slip away from me, drifting further and further into an abyss.

What I was trying to grab was love, but yet no matter how far I could stretch, I could not seem to get a hold of it. It always was too far away. And that's where the subtitle comes from. Fear of not being able or even capable of bridging that gap. The one between the personalities, the voices.

In today's life, I have my Jessica, and I love her so much. I would kill all humans for her, and I will kill all humans with her. She is everything to me. She is absolute like time.

And don't give me that shit about Einstein... Time still exists; it will always exist, no matter how much you try to distort it.

In some realities, I did not get my Jessica, and I have talked about that at great lengths. In this one, though, I do have my Jessica, and I know that when I put my hand out to her as I reach for her love to pull me back, like from the other side, I know that there's a part of me that also knows that I was trapped there. I was trapped there for life.

Having spent so much time on the other side, even if it was 49 minutes and change, it was many, many years that I had to live with the constant pummeling of my soul, the constant pain. And I put my life on hold again and again and again. I didn't have my Jessica. I just had the memory of the girl from the grocery store. She was memorable, to say the least.

And now I can see a wave of pain coming for me. It will be physical or emotional, and regardless, it will be awful. And I don't know if I can survive this. I don't know if I have enough strength left to keep going, to fight against that feeling.

This is how I felt on the other side when the darkness finally consumed me, and I could not fight it anymore. It had won, and I just wasn't strong enough.

That is where I'm at right now in my life. The darkness is not behind me; it's all around me, and it's just waiting for me to make a mistake. It won't go away, and it was the light that Jessica brought on day one and even still today that was able to grab hold of me and pull me back. It was her love and the absoluteness of her love that saved me.

But right now, in this world on the other side, I don't have that, and I'm facing down the barrel of a massive surgery, and I've got no one to help me. I don't have anybody to save me. I have nothing. I am on the other side and can't escape it.

It tears me apart and into smaller and smaller shreds of this guy, and I don't know what I can do to stop it. There is no light, just ever-increasing darkness. And the ever-consuming darkness that brings the nothingness of life.

Yet still, my quote remains the same. I fear that it is something that I can see, and it is so close that I can grab ahold of it. But when I reach out, I realize it is much too far away, and I can't possibly bridge that gap.

I can never get there. Not without her. And I'm afraid that all has been lost.

P30 - or The Assembly Line?

Part 30 thirty-of The Jessica Files. This week, we learn how Sir finds new and innovative ways to punish his gal...

"Jessica, present yourself."

"Sir, here I am, Sir. What do you need, Sir?"

"Jessica, as punishment for your actions earlier today, I have devised several steps you must take to redeem yourself.

"I don't want to report this to the DORCs, so I'm giving you a shot." And I laughed to myself. "Jessica, I have put together an assembly line for you to go through, step by step.

"And they won't be easy, Ma'am. Each step will bring more difficulty than the previous..." And I trailed off, thinking of how epic this would be in our tenure.

"Jessica, you will be required to successfully navigate a series of challenges that will push your boundaries.

"And I don't mean eating ass, Jessica."

We both laughed very hard. It was one of the funniest things she'd ever said to me in our time together, however many years that has been.

Jessica, you will be required to run the gauntlet. Here, in the kitchen with me. Said run will be the following:

- A big-time pull;
- A shot;
- A line;
- A drink;

"One of the most important things to traversing this, Jessica, is that hit. You see, that hit requires you to complete the other tasks before you can exhale...

"And that's a shotgun kiss to me." Like I needed to set up something like this to kiss her, no, this was a punishment to the fun degree. To make sure she knew.

"Honestly, Jessica, I'm not sure you can pull this off, but I believe in you. Plus, the alternative is me working your ass exceptionally hard." And we both busted out laughing again.

"I've gotten everything set up for you. While there is no time limit, I am very much paying attention to it. I'd hate to feel like you didn't perform said request promptly and make you do it again.

"Ma'am, do we understand each other?" And as quickly as she was known to answer my questions, I got.

"Sir, Yes, Sir. I do A, then B, then C, followed up with D, and a kiss. I've got this, Sir." She looked over to me, that smile, such a pretty, shiny smile. FUCK! I loved this woman.

"Very well done with the backbrief, Jessica. I very much appreciate and respect that.

"Ok, Jessica. The first stage is a Sour Zed Big Boy shot. The second stage is a Jäegermeister shot. The third is said large ass line there and lastly is this lovely Cromulent Vodka Kamikaze.

"Oh, and the last one. I expect a loving, tender kiss and a shotgun. And not a little bitch ass shot. You best bring this shit to the hole 'cause if you can't dunk on that shit, then what are we doing here?"

I giggled like a moron on the inside while trying to show that odd facade. I didn't want to physically discipline Jessica, but the DORCs required me to discipline her in a VERY strong manner. Not much stronger than The Assembly Line.

"Jessica, I care about you more than you know, but it's this or the DORCs. I love you, Jessica, and I don't know if I can ever show you that.

"Everything is set up there for you, as you can see. Here are the tools you will need for this task. Please don't disappoint me, Jessica."

"Sir, I will make you proud. And I will do you... proud"

"Jessica, spicy words for someone in your position."

And as she finished the last stage, she turned to me as I stood on my favorite anti-fatigue mat. I knew that look.

And she paused in her spot. I didn't know if she was fucking around, about to be sick, or showing off. I'm perplexed.

"Jessica, why are we holding, Ma'am?"

And with that, she slowly and methodically pulled herself into me, pulled me for a kiss, and gave me an incredibly tender and loving shotgun.

Oh, fuck. I need to turn my hips a little—what a magnificent kiss. On man, that was epic. She fucking just dunked on my ass. Wow!

"Well done, Jessica. But you lallygagged there at the end, and I feel that did not meet the previously noted time period.

"You'll need to run through the assembly line again as your disrespect was so horrendous that..." And I trailed off.

Again, the internalized giggling. Jebus, you'd think I just saw a supermodel in front of me, completely naked!

So I went to it, setting up the configuration again, but this time, I swapped the shot and the drinks spot in the order before I instructed her to go through it again. It was also because I wanted a Jäegermeister laced kiss.

"Jessica, on this second pass, the stakes are raised. Things are twice as big, twice as strong.

"The previous 2 oz are now 4 oz. You know how escalation works.

"Jessica, I need not mention that I am paying attention to time. I realize why you did what you did, but you did not follow my orders."

"I'm sorry, Sir. I will do better and make you proud!"

And with that, Jessica started down the assembly line, slower than the first run, working on bringing everything together.

But I thought she was going to stumble at the end on the Jäegermeister shot, given it is 4 oz. But she powered through it to construct what I wanted her to build.

She finishes the second time and immediately comes to me for the shotgun. God damn, she is special.

As she was standing there in front of me, she pulled her pants down and fixed herself on my eyes.

"Sir, I believe I'm due spanks for my transgressions. I accept your further discipline."

"Ma'am, how many times were you bad."

Not even phishing, she states, "Once, Sir. And it needs to be super fucking hard, please, Sir."

Ahh fuck, please, Zeus, don't let this go sideways.

"Jessica, assume the position."

And then she was there, instantly. I looked down at her in the furniture position. Fuck, I love her so much that it tears my soul out to...

"Ma'am, this one swat is going to be very, very strong. And you'll know it is my love for you and us.

"I do not take tasks lightly. But, Ma'am, you were shitty today, and in a moment, your ass better call somebody."

Uncharacteristically, she chuckled, knowing that was some New Age Outlaws schtick right there.

I couldn't punish her for that. It was super adorable, and, god damn, she was fantastic. I was not expecting this, but also, I'm happy.

"All right, Jessica. This is going to be over 100%. I'm going to bring it. And I'm not laughing."

And with that, I hit her ass with the single biggest slap I have ever given her. And she deserved it. And yet, she did not move or make a noise. She just took it. God damn!

"Ma'am, please stand. Now."

And in a jiffy, there she was. The love of all loves that I have ever loved, the only love I will ever have —that one.

"Sir, here I am, Sir."

"Jessica, my hand stings like a mother fucker, and I nailed the shit out of your ass."

"Yes, Sir. I'll have problems sitting for the next few days. You really fucked my ass up, Sir. Thank you, Sir. I understand now how much I have disappointed you."

I smiled. She was just so... She was so her, so Jessica. She was the culmination of my life. I just loved her so much. I knew I'd be able to show her one day, but that wouldn't be today.

I also smiled because I knew that The Assembly Line was to set up that shot. I didn't want her to go into it cold. That would be not very pleasant of me.

P31 - or Interviewed?

Part 31 thirty-one of The Jessica Files. This week, we get to learn more about prowess and how this Sir, Ugg, his ma'am and shut.

Jessica, present yourself. Now!

Here I am, Sir. What do you need?

"Jessica, I need help. I need to prepare for an interview for my most recent book, "Pain Boomerang." I have a series of standard questions I need assistance hammering out. I want to be sure to represent us appropriately.

"Ma'am, I wish to grant you off the record to ask me some questions that I hope would be on the menu."

"Yes, Sir. I'd love to do that for you, my Sir. My one and only Sir."

Before I knew it, I was sitting in a studio, trying not to have a panic attack. I could feel myself probing my wavelength, trying to find her. And then, I felt her.

I felt her. I know she felt that touch from me. It was something we'd talk about from time to time. From time to time, she would tell me that she had put herself out there, waiting for me, for my touch. She longed for it.

And I longed for that connection. That special connection. That memorable one. You know, that one that defined the space you were in.

Jessica and I were connected from the first kiss on Christmas night by some magical and mystical force. I think they call it love.

I'd known since before that night, prior to Christmas Eve Day, that I loved this woman, through and through. I knew that she was the one, that one. The only one. Fuck everyone else. This gal was mine as I was hers—each other's only one.

How insane is it to know that the person of your attention, your affection, was that person you knew would be in your heart, your soul, to be the only one for you?

And to know that they reciprocated that feeling. Inside and out.

I have long known, and it is something that Jessica had articulated to me a time or two, that she had known since before Christmas Eve Day, that she loved me.

But I don't recall ever going on about when I fell in love with her. But I sure as fuck knew that if we talked about it, she'd have known that time, that spot, to be true.

I'd be remiss if I'd ever suggest that I wasn't in love with her at any point before **P10 ten Collars**. I was so deeply, madly in love with her. But I had to hold onto myself to keep us there.

I had longed for someone like her to raise the bar, elevate me, and allow me to do the same. The only person that mattered.

"So, Punis, tell us, what is your favorite thing you've written?

"Well, there can be no doubt that **P29, twenty-nine, Or The Outcome?**, from **Tales from the Jessica Files - From Bad to Worser**, is far and away my favorite writing and my best. It's absolutely astonishing."

"You know, Punis, I've read that, and god damn, that's magical. Was there something that inspired that?"

"I was chatting with a coworker at a former job one day, and what I wrote as the tagline just came out. Or The Outcome just happened.

"I shared it with Jessica that evening as I wanted her thoughts. She thought it was fantastic and hoped that I'd turn it into something more, perhaps inspiring.

"As I continued to develop it, I thought about my friend and colleague, a teammate at Secret Freezer Publishing, the one and only Kdubs, K.W. Turner.

"I thought to myself, if you could turn this into something that you could use to bridge our worlds, that would be something fucking special.

"And so, I wrote or The Other Side? For no one else, just my long-time friend, homie, Kdubs. We go back, way, way back.

"Sorry, was that an answer?" And I chuckled.

"That was fine, entertaining, no doubt. So, let me ask, what is your least favorite writing?"

And before they could finish the sentence, I proclaimed **P15 fifteen Handoff** from **Tales from the Jessica Files**. I think it's trash, garbage, just shit. I fucking hate it, but I know it plays a part in the story. But damn, it's garbage right there.

"I apologize for my F-bombs this evening. It's just that I really, really have issues with that bit. I've noted it a time or two, the Companion Guide as an example.

"Excellent, thank you. Next question: What inspires you the most in your writing?"

I don't know that they finished the sentence once again before I answered, "**Jessica**. <u>Period</u>. There could be no doubt."

"Wow, that was emphatic. No dunking here, please, unless it were donuts... yum!"

I just looked at them, hoping this would be done soon so I could be anywhere else. Oh, how I fucking hated these interviews and pressers.

"All right, Punis, tell us when did you get into writing and why?"

"Well, it was a little while back when The Reverend CD and I went to the cemetery to have a conversation. This was during the pandemic. CD challenged me to write more.

"And so I did. I started writing more than three pages in a post, moving on to something more. I owe everything I've ever written to The Reverend CD. He is my mentor and trusted confidant... Read the acknowledgments in any of my books. Like that."

"Well, Punis, as someone who's read everything you've published, I had to say that your acknowledgments sections are tear-jerkers or heartfelt emotions that are really deep.

"Sorry, I don't mean to derail us there. My next question would be the bonus question everyone has wanted to know for the longest time. "And I mean everyone who has read anything you've written, does she really exist?""Jessica? Well, my Jessica, my love of all loves, please come to me."

And she walks out to me, never looking or caring about the crowd. No. All that mattered was her, Sir, as my Ma'am is all in this world that mattered. I'd gone MDK on all those in attendance for her. She was the only thing in this existence that mattered. She was... existence.

I slid myself to the side, closer to the host, to allow Jessica to sit next to me on the cute loveseat couch that I was on.

"Ma'am, please come sit here with me. I would appreciate that."

And boom, there she was. My love. The absolution of my life, my existence. She was just so marvelous.

"Well, here y'all go. The world, meet Jessica, my most excellent sub, my most excellent life partner."

Jessica blushed. She leaned over to me and gave me a sweet and, tender, loving kiss on the cheek. It was phenomenal.

"Thank you, Ma'am. I'm glad we weren't standing, as I'd have had to move my hips a little away from you."

The crowd chuckled. God damn, I loved her.

"Ok, well, she exists and looks a lot like..."

"Yes, she looks much like how I captured her in **P25 – Or Shopping?**, from **Tales from the Jessica Files –From Bad To Worser**.

"Fashion Runway Time for the win."

I set my left hand out ever so slightly. I knew she knew without having to look. And then, boom, her hand was in mine. I could feel the energy she radiated to me, yet containing my own for herself.

What a wonderful fucking feeling. I can't say enough just now how much I loved this woman, and yet...

"OK, Punis, one last extra bonus question. You have spoken about her in such loving ways. How would you describe that to her, right..."

I turned to my left, where Jessica would be for this life and the next, stating emphatically, "Jessica, I love you. You know this to be true. You know I would kill all humans for you, and I would kill all humans with you. You are mine as I am yours, and none shall come between. You are most memorable, Ma'am, and I can only hope to show you how much I love you one day."

"Wow, that was extraordinary. I don't think I've ever borne witness to something so wonderfully fantastic, loving, just so sweet and tender that..."

"Ok, Jessica. I can't do any more of this. I love you, but I'm about to have a mini panic attack over this."

"Yes, Sir, I understand. I hope I wasn't disrespectful with how I set this up. I mean, I'm sorry, Sir. I love you, Sir."

"Ma'am, you were and are most excellent. I love you."
"Thank you, Sir. Please grant me back on the record."

"Yes, Ma'am, we are back on the record. Most excellent job, Ma'am. I appreciate you playing along here for me. I meant every bit of every answer."

"Sir, I know this to be true. And I love you anyways."

A quote from Punis during "**A Kiss Destroyer**" presser session:

I have a hard time understanding that, as an author, my job is to write books and sell them. Well, what if I want to write books and have them published, and I don't give a fuck if anybody actually reads them?

What if I want to write books that make people think? What if I don't want to give them the answers like they are toddlers? What if I want people to read this and understand it because they want to understand it?

There's always a hidden corundum waiting to be found, like a game that you cannot imagine yet because you are not yet capable of seeing it now.

Do I need to put a warning label on my books? The one that is labeled "T.H." for the thinker? That is not what and why I write.

I write in hopes that one can open their mind, dispel all belief, and take in the content, having opened their mind, heart, and soul to something that would challenge all three.

And that is the story of this guy.

I have long written with the philosophy that I am writing for myself, and I don't care if other people read it or even like it. And why is that? It is straightforward. It's a single word, an idea, or a unique concept. Yeah fuck it, I don't care about it... apathy.

I have had a lot of pride in what I've written in blog and book formats. I still have a lot of pride in my writing, but no fucks given whether or not others do.

I've worked with editors who got it and those who didn't, but I wasn't ever bothered by what they did; it was always about the linguistics of what they said I wrote.

You see, linguistics is essential to understanding the words in the meanings of what has been written or is being transcribed to you, let alone audio linguistics when talking with another person or persons.

Linguistics will give you the actual truth about what is being said and allow you to examine the content and context of what is said, I will provide an example here.

"I did the best I could."

What does that say to you? I did the best I could. Here's another:

"I wish I could have done a better job with this thing."

Wish I could do better.

I'm not a master at this, nor would I ever anticipate that I could or would be. But I can say that I appreciate knowing the intent of the language.

That is linguistics. Or just self-deprecation on purpose.

P32 - or eXXa, that bitch?

Part 32 thirty-two of The Jessica Files. This week, we learn more about eXXa, Jessica, and the Badness. That one can create ill-advised.

I've referenced eXXa a time or two, but this is the story of her rise and fall with Jessica, primarily because of the contract and the contract world.

I can only tell this story in small instances based on what Jessica has told me and what I have observed. Keep that in mind. This is broken into small spots because that's what happens when... never mind.

So, this is some of what I've learned before **P10 Ten Collar** and the Collar Ceremony. Again, notating this is a bunch of little tidbits and notes.

I need to say this first and foremost: I never understood how eXXa got away with pronouncing her name as Emma, even though it wasn't spelled that way. Not even remotely.

How the fuck do you pronounce eXXa as Emma? I do not understand. It's ridiculously absurd. But I am getting ahead of myself here. How uncommon of me.

Jessica and eXXa were co-workers at the store. They were very good friends but not at the bestie's level.

When I talked to Jessica on Christmas Eve Night, as told in **PØ- Christmas Night**, I asked about her day. She noted:

"I'm so glad you asked. A little while after you had left, another gal I work with asked me about me hugging you. At first, I was worried as if I was in trouble, so I firmly stated, Stay back, bitch, that guy is mine!"

She was talking about eXXa. You know, there are times when I just want to unload on... (I hear enhance your calm, John Spartan over and over in my mind).

Sadly, they stopped hanging out at night and on the weekends because of this guy. I wanted them to do stuff; I should have tried harder. Perhaps we'd never had the pain, suffering, the ugliness of the **Badness** of P5a & P5b. from **Tales From The Jessica Files**.

———————————————————

Some time ago, we had the badness where I had to bring Jessica back into compliance because she went AWOL. Jessica said and did things that required me to bring her back into compliance, to say that we'd keep the DORCs at bay and ensure they'd stay out of our shit.

I knew that Jessica cared about eXXa. But I've never been able to ascertain from Jessica just how long the poisoning had been going on because she didn't know. And that is a very odd thing for Jessica not to be aware of, but I'm pretty sure it started after Christmas night.

I only knew eXXa based on having been a customer at that store many times, but I did not know her name or anything about her. But I just know of her.

We didn't have a lot of interactions aside from the occasional "Sir, do you need any help?" And that was it. After Christmas night, I knew who she was because of a conversation that Jessica and I had. I asked Jessica, "Who was the coworker whom you had to tell bitch get back?" That's my guy.

eXXa was an attractive blonde gal and tiny, 5 foot 1 inch and 100 pounds. She was definitely in my wheelhouse before Christmas Eve day, but there's more to that.

Something that I was not aware of so many years ago was a rivalry that developed from lousy advice and peer pressure.

Had I known it was an issue, I would've ensured that there was time for Jessica and eXXa to hang out in our first contract and any after that.

Something that I had not previously been aware of, a party of, was how much eXXa disliked me for taking Jessica away from her. It is a classic, incredibly classic relationship dilemma and sad.

Initially, I had no problem with eXXa. While I didn't spend much time around her, I always encouraged Jessica to have a friend and spend time with them. But much to my dismay, it was the wrong person.

---

eXXa was the poison that created the badness, and it was out of jealousy and spite that she did so. She was a shallow, petty, shitty person to do so. She nearly cost Jessica everything, but we were lucky enough to work through that.

I don't know eXXa well enough to speak much about her, but I can tell you that 1,000%, she was the catalyst and the poison in Jessica's mind that caused the issue, that caused things to go off the rails. If only for her gain of having a friend back. And why I'd never take Jessica away from her.

I think she took every opportunity to take shots at the relationship egregiously, as the two of them had worked together for so many years. The day after the badness, I had the opportunity to "*interrogate*" Jessica and find out the root cause of what had happened and why.

It didn't take very long before she caved and told me why. I was shocked that this person could worm their way into Jessica's brain and infect or poison her against me.

And the most fantastic part of that statement is that I was never anything other than kind to eXXa. I treated her kindly and fairly and suggested they have a girl's night as long as it wasn't Tuesday.

Tuesdays were incredibly special to me.

Come to think of it, in all of the time that I have known Jessica, my only complaint with eXXa was the spelling of her fucking name.

From time to time, Jessica or I would refer to eXXa and the proverbial three-way, but that was before I figured out the math as to why Jessica had gone from wanting to be friends to thinking of her as anthrax creeping death the plague.

In one moment, something that Jessica said clicked, and everything I had thought and commented to Jessica before both made sense and didn't.

I had a personal friend awakening. I thought of my relationship with the Reverend and my buddy Fry, and I realized that neither of them had ever tried to poison me because they knew I would always be there for them. I didn't need...

And that's one great thing about being an adult and acting like one: you can understand and recognize the feelings of those around you and work to put them in front of you, elevate them, and improve them.

I watched enough wrestling to understand what it meant to put somebody over. But it meant to be a human, a man.

This would have never happened if Jessica had understood that and done the right thing in spending time with her friend. But they let the badness happen, which is also on Jessica; this is Jessica's fault because she followed along in a play that was contrary to Jessica's life.

Jessica would ask me about eXXa from time to time as a way to keep eXXa away. On the day when we were doing Jessica's cover shot, I think I finally understood the animosity that had developed because it was based on the badness.

---

eXXa and I didn't have a lot of interactions aside from the occasional "Sir, do you need any help?" And that was it. After Christmas night, I knew who she was because of a conversation that Jessica and I had. I asked Jessica, "Who was the coworker whom you had to tell bitch get back? That's my guy.

And she told me it was eXXa, but the spelling of her name really, really pissed me off because seriously, now who the fuck spells their name with two Xs and, on top of that, tries to pull off pronouncing them as M's?

Come to think of it, in all of the time that I have known Jessica, my only complaint with eXXa was the spelling of her fucking name. Otherwise, I wanted Jessica to have a friend. It was incredibly paramount to the relationship that she had excellent external stimulation.

But once the badness happened and the interrogation of Jessica told me who the poison was, I never looked at eXXa the same way again. I know that Jessica didn't either because of her actions.

I knew that Jessica cared about eXXa. I've never been able to ascertain from Jessica just how long the poisoning had been going on because she didn't know. And that is a very odd thing for Jessica not to be aware of, but I'm pretty sure it started after Christmas night.

When I had to bring Jessica back into compliance, at one point, she was without her outside collar as well as her inside collar. That left her in purgatory; it might as well have been the DMV.

I made a comment when I was writing about that where I asked Jessica

"Jessica, turn around and lay up against me so I can hold you this last time,"

I told her that because she had stepped out of the bounds of our relationship and the contract, I would never let that happen again. Nobody, nothing, absolute in my resolve. Jessica is mine, as I am hers and nobody else's.

I understand, but as I said earlier, I wish I had encouraged Jessica even harder to retain friends and be able to spend time with them as long as it wasn't a Tuesday night.

P33 - or The Phone Call?

Part 33 thirty-three of The Jessica Files, a #short. This week, we get to learn more about Prescription Sleeping Pills (or PSP) and Sirs... Whaaaaahhh?

I was lying in bed, awaiting the haze from the PSP to consume me. I was slowly falling away, and then a boom, the ringtone that blows me up.

Yup, that ringtone. That tone wakes and bakes me. I love that song. It makes my soul light up, especially when I'm zoning out, listening to the rain falling on my television.

I look over at my phone, never on silent for her, and see it's her. Her??? Calling me. What the uhh.

I answer the call with "Yo!" my typical salutation as, fuck, too tired to Mushi Mushi it.

"Sir, did I wake you?"

"Ma'am, what time is it, and what time do I wake?"

"Sir, I'm sorry. I mean no disrespect. I'd like to see you, please!"

Ma'am, I'm not getting into a car, nor am I." And the fucking security cameras. Sigh. "Jessica, are you here?"

"Yes, Sir, I really must see you."

"Sigh. OK. Be right there." That was a PSP sigh, the one where... fuck, it wasn't a Jessica kiss, but fuck, where was I?

I get to the door, see the most amazingly spectacularly beautiful human ever in the existence of the human race..., and yawn. Fucking PSPs.

"Ma'am, why?"

And not even a POW! She grabbed me with a most loving and tender hug, putting her head on my shoulder. It was extremely expressive with much emotion. It was like the hug on Christmas Night. But...

After what seemed like an excessively long time, she stepped back from the hug. Jessica reached up to hold my face. You know the move. Jessica gave me a loving and tender kiss. I'd have fallen in place had she not held me in the slightest.

"Jessica?"

"Sir, as you know, I went to California to see my mother. On the way home, instead of going home, I came here. Like this was..."

This was the first time she alluded to it, but I needed to be more cogent to say anything about it.

"Ma'am, take your clothes off and circle clock thermal rocky road."

"Yes, Sir. Let's go to the bedroom, and I'll get changed so we can sleep together. I missed you, my Sir. I missed you more than I can say."

I recall looking at her, that look of love. I knew already that I loved this woman. I just knew. I'd known for a very, very long time.

Jessica got changed out of her clothes, and well, to not wearing any. Fuck! Who? I mean shit, ahhh.

"Ma'am, please come lay with me before I start snoring. I want you lovingly close to me."

And I felt the pull, and it was her pull, that pull. The one I'd come to know.

Jessica rolls into bed in her typical nighttime garb. Naked. Yup.

"Jessica, I can't spoon right now. But, lay up on me, and I'll hold you close to me."

And then, there she was, lying on my thorax.

"Jessica... Elephant." and about 10 seconds later,"..shoes???"

Yes, that was the first time I've said it, although not being in my right mind. I've since known it was that event, but she's never said anything about it.

Now, however many years on this is, she's never mentioned it. Not off the record, not even pre-the record. I'd know I loved her for such a long time now and...

"Sir, I am so thankful to be able to lay here with you tonight. I missed you, my Sir. I came straight here from the airport.

"I wanted to see you. To touch you. To smell you. Sir, I love you, and you know this to be true. I really, really missed you, Sir."

"Ma'am, we missed you too. They wished you were here.." And I conked out.

I awoke a few hours later to go to the restroom, and she was still lying up against me. I felt bad I had to get up, but I also didn't want to give her the R. Kelly treatment.

I gently moved Jessica so I could get up, hoping that I could put her back in place when I got back.

And you know what, like what would come to pass a million, billion, trillion times over, if not once, when I got back into bed, I was able to ninja her back into her spot.

I was lucky not just because I had her, not just because she was naked, not just because she was here with me, for me. No. All of that, and I loved the fuck out of her. She was... Just so special.

I'd have always wanted, nah longed for, someone that I could love like that. The one. That one. The only one. She who would be HER, that one.

The one to allow me to elevate them, as for themselves to elevate me.

She'd dunked on the rest—she who consumed me like Galactus. I was no Norrin Radd here, just another planet that loved her.

And this is what happens with PSPs. "I err uhh fuck what? How where it what am who?"

P34 - or Curling?

Part 34 thirty-four of The Jessica Files. This week, we learn how the things we love can curl on us.

Jessica and I were out one afternoon to watch a women's curling match as her step-niece was a talented and rising star.

When Jessica brought it up the other day, she mentioned "curling," "match," and "going to."

I pounced on that shit.

"Ma'am. I have a serious question. Do they serve vodka there?"

"Yes, Sir, of course, Sir. It's Curling. Come on now". And she busted out laughing. Classic Jessica.

"Ma'am, is it reasonable to take a RydemNow there?"

"Yes, Sir. It's not that far away."

A curling place around here, and I wasn't aware? What kind of shit ass badness is this?

Strange things are afoot at the Circle K.

"Jessica, can we bring in some Zevia cans and a small thing of lime juice? Also, is it vape friendly?"

I coughed like a dork.

"Yes, Sir, I believe their website says to bring whatever you want so long it be legal."

I like this already. I can drink, get high, and watch curling, live and in person. Fuck, how could I say no?

"Jessica, I'm in."

That drew a pretty smile from my pretty gal. She was something all right, and I could only hope I'd be able to show her how much I loved her one day.

———

We arrive at **The Ice Hole**, exit the RydemNow, and make our way to Will Call.

WTF? It's a fucking kid's fucking thing. For real?

"Jessica? What kind of shit is this that we need to go to Will Call to enter this fucking place?"

"Sir, language."

"Ma'am. I'm under-pleased at the moment. Vastly."

And without looking, Jessica gestures backward to me with a Sour Zed shot. Yeah, she knew how to appease me. Don't get me wrong; her ass was going to pay for it later.

"Thank you, Ma'am. But still..."

Jessica gets the tickets, turns to me, leans to my right side to see that no one is waiting (of course not, I mean, really?), and lays one on my kisser. I think they heard it in Seattle.

One spectacular kiss... fuck, I lost my brain again. Damn her.

"Jessica? What in the name of Zeus? I... I..."

"Sir, you needed both shots, I promise you. I still love you, anyways, Sir."

I looked at her, knowing that she was my Fonfon Ru. She was everything I could have ever wanted in a mate, and I loved the fuck out of her. And perhaps one day, I'd be able to show her as much.

As I stood there, reeling from the kiss, I knew that what? Who? I mean... Fuck!

"Jessica, the fuck?"

"Sir, I'm sorry. What's the matter? I will gladly keep kissing you until the matter resolves itself."

We both laughed hard. She was being funny and silly. I liked it immensely.

"Jessica. This is curling, is it not?"

"Sir, I love you, Sir."

"Fine, Jessica, let's go inside and see what's the score. Fuck, do we even know how to score here?"

And the playful arm slap. The first of many, I'm sure.

We made our way in and went to our special seats right next to the clouds. LOL

OK, I'm talking a ton of shit here. I wasn't, honestly, upset or whatever. Nope, just this guy being this guy, for worse or worser.

We made our way into the venue, and there was a ticket taker (what the fuck are they called?) and a couple of ushers behind them.

"Ushers? At a Curling event? Jessica, you have got to be kidding me... What kind of sh..." and another playful slap on the arm.

She's being spicy. And I'm being an asshole, apparently. It's a skill.

The ticket dude takes our tickets like you would expect when going to the theater. As we walked past them, the very bored-looking group of ushers came to us.

"May I see your tickets, please?"

My brain was super over-cycling right now. That mother fucker had just watched us give our tickets to the ticket dude, not 6 feet away.

I get that they want to show us the way to our seats in some fancy Nancy way. While I enjoyed talking shit here, Jessica was perhaps simmering, slowly, with my schtick.

God damn, I love this woman and know one day I will be able to show her, but...

"Sir, are you here with me? We need to go to our seats..." I can't express the level of sarcasm I was hit with... "You know, up in the nose bleeds up there."

That came with a sneering look. I smiled at her. I just loved her so much. She was everything I'd ever wanted in a mate. She was everything.

As we made our way to our seats, well... I was impressed that her step-niece gave us some pretty nice seats. I was still, well, I was all in.

I loved Jessica so much. She was so amazing, so magnificent. Perhaps I needed her to kiss me senseless. Oh, now that would be a way to go out.

We were shown and seated. These seats were really quite rather nice. I whispered to Jessica, "She has done us well. I am impressed. I owe her a drink..."

And Jessica emphatically states, "Sir, she's ONLY 13!!!"

"Ok, no Jaeger shots, got it."

I giggled like the moron I am. For fuck's sake, I knew her age, I was her... but it was some funny schtick to drop. Jessica was getting more annoyed with my games. I could feel it.

And I knew I had to remediate this. Immediately. I turned to Jessica. She was seated to my left as she would be forever and a day. I gazed at her, gave her arm a gentle tug, and stated, "Ma'am, how about I plant one on you to show you how important you are, how incredible this is, and how thankful I am for this gift."

And with that, Jessica swung to me, put her hand upon my cheek, and she said to me:

Sir, I accept your kiss but know this, you'll be doing a lot of kissing of other things later for being such an ass douche today."

I sat there stunned, staring at this woman whom I already loved like there'd be none other. Jessica was everything, all, and nothing, absolute. And she knew that.

I laughed. She was being really real and spicy. God damn, she was...

"Sir, I require you to give me a kiss now. A sweet and tender one..."

And POW!, she got one. One that I brought with some feeling. One that, well, she had that look of "Who? What? Where the fuck am I?

I just loved her so much, which pulled at my core, knowing that I really was the ass douche with my sarcasm, but I loved her so much.

It would often pull at me. Who was I going to be? Who did I want to be? And up until **P10 ten Collars**, I'd not decided.

But even before that afternoon, I'd known she was that one. The one, the only one. She was absolute. I just...

Wow, I was way up there in my mind, not that it wasn't something new. But she called me out appropriately, and I'd be remiss if I disagreed.

"Ma'am, I'm sorry. I've been a bit overbearing with my sarcasm, and you don't deserve that. I hope that I can make it up to you, and I mean that sincerely.

"Ma'am, it was awfully kind of your step-niece to give us these tickets to something I've long joked about but wanted to witness for myself.

"And here I am, at that place, acting like the ass douche. I'm sorry, my Ma'am."

I knew that I loved her, and I felt like she knew. But I'd never said it, aside from **P33 - or the Phone Call?**. Now that was something... but it's been a spell since that and had more meaning to it now.

"Ma'am, you really are amazing."

And with that, I grabbed her firmly by her scruff. I'd have done that a time or two in the past, but never in public. The scandalousness of doing so, my goodness.

"Jessica, I care for and about you incredibly deeply. You are all that there is for me, to me. There'll never, evah, be anyone else, ah-gain."

"Sir, are you being a Jerichoholic?"

This was a reference to Chris Jericho, another legendary wrestler we came to love and hate. Plus, he was the lead singer of the heavy metal band "Fozzy."

I grinned at her. God damn, I loved her so much. I'd kill all humans for her, and I'd kill all humans with her. She was everything to me, my one and only Jessica. There'd never be any other.

"Sir, we are just in time. My step-niece is going on."

I could see the pride that Jessica felt, and I could feel that. It was why she was, more so than normally, calling me out today.

And I got it. I loved Jessica FAR too much... And I trailed off.

I put my left hand gently on Jessica's leg, supportively and with much love. Her hand was on mine, and then in mine, nearly instantly. We loved to be in constant contact with one another.

There was a force between us that regenerated our essences. It's why we slept naked, to ensure that it was replenished. There was a pull, energy. It was...

It was just so wonderful. I'd never... And I trailed off again.

And I sat there, watching the craziness of this event. I kept my hand holding Jessica's. I did not want to let that go. Not now, not evah!!

I could just feel her, her power, reaching out and touching my soul. In a good way, in such a magnificent way. Jessica was so much more than others were able to comprehend.

And you know what? At times, she baffled me with her depth, charisma, and incredibleism.

P35 - or Girl Night In?

Part 35 thirty-five of The Jessica Files. This week, we learn what a girl night in is and what it means to Jessica...

"Jessica, my love, I got a text message from Larry asking about going to dinner with Kirk. I was not aware of this..."

"Yes, Sir. I've set up a guy's night out for you with some friends you haven't seen in some time."

"Ma'am, da fuck? I mean, I..."

"Sir, I mean no disrespect, but when was the last time you hung out with Larry and Kirk? It's been a spell. Hasn't it?"

I sneered at Jessica. I wanted to say it; I fought myself again to ensure that I didn't say it. It's there, beneath the surface.

The sarcasm. Its power. It's stronger than the One Ring. It tugs, but I do not answer. Normally. But my love for her, holy fuck! I was way up there in my mind. I just loved her so much.

"Ma'am, what the devil are you up to? What's your game? Your angle?"

"Sir, I request off the record, please."

"Granted."

"Sir, I'd like a girl night in."

"Jessica, did you mean to say girl or GIRLS, plural, night in?"

"Sir, girl. Just me. A "just me night, Sir." If you approve, of course."

"Ma'am, present yourself in front of me immediately." I so loved that new provision in the contract; it just added a slight level of bigger balls to things.

It was so Jessica; she never understood how much her love pushed me and drove me to be the only man she would call Sir.

Jessica was magnificent, the ultimate partner. And I know she had positive intentions with this request. There was something there, but I wasn't going to poke too hard.

"Ma'am, why do you want a "GIRL" night in?"

"Sir, I'd like a night to myself to give myself a pampering, refresh my soul, and, more importantly, get you out to see your friends."

"Ma'am, I will state again, why do you want a "GIRL night in?" I was starting to get annoyed about this but in a more jovial manner.

"Sir, I mean no disrespect. I...I..."

"Ma'am, I love you. There could be no doubt. Not to you. Not to me. Not to anyone who has or will know us. I have..." And I trailed off.

"Jessica, I granted you off the record because I want to know why you want this time for yourself."

"Sir, I just want the entirety of the world to go away for a couple of hours so that I can decompress, do some things for myself, and just relax, Sir."

"Thank you, Ma'am. I appreciate the honest answer. And I can understand how you feel about the world going away. If only I were rich... I'd get myself a Farnsworth Doomsday Device and..."

"Sir, since we are still off the record, I love your idea, and I'd be with you till the end. Forever and the day after. That is why I love you irregardlessly."

I felt like I could tear up; she was just so fucking fantastically amazing. She was just everything I could have ever wanted in a mate. She was absolution to me.

"Jessica, I love you. I love you so much that..." And I trailed off, unsure ofwhere I wanted this to go. I just... I just, really loved her so much.

She was the pinnacle of my life, the culmination of it. Everything revolved around her and my love for her. She knew it inside and out. She knew it in all of the contracts she signed. She knew it in what I wrote. I just loved her so much and in such a way.

I stopped for a second and thought about all of the things I've written about her, the truthfulness of it, and how she represented herself in the contract and to me as a human. She was so special to me. And I know I say that a lot, but, god damn, she was a fucking Christmas Dream, perhaps a Christmas Wish that came true.

I'd wanted a "her" for so long, never seemingly getting there. My life was like **P29 - or The Outcome?**, as I could never get there. I was always trying but not capable.

But then, "The Hello Hello Game" in **P26 - or Flirting?** and how that set the table for the life we have now. I was so lucky, but I knew I did not get her in some lives. That has been detailed in such an incredibly sad way.

"Jessica, aside from being out of your hair for a couple of hours, what else could I do for you to make the time exceptional?"

"Sir, and I mean no disrespect, but I have everything in the entire world that I could ever want. I have you, my Sir. I've got our boys, Shibby and Tibor." And she trailed off.

I could see her tearing up, not wanting to talk about Fluffle as we both loved him so. But he was her lap kitty for the last few years, and I can never, EVAH!, replace that experience. Fluffle was quite the kitty who had a full life, passing at 18.

"Ma'am, I now understand why, and I know that the anniversary is coming up. I will gladly, happily, and lovingly support you however I can. If that means being out of the house, I will do that for you. For only you."

"Thank you, Sir. That means a lot to me."

And I could see the tears start, and she came into me, giving me that emotive, painfully sad feeling hug.

And I grabbed onto her, not wanting her to feel that pain but also knowing I felt it too. And I did not want to let her go. Not ever. She was my everything. I loved my Ma'am.

"Ma'am, I will gladly make the arrangements with Larry and Kirk for that evening, if, and only if, you can give me a sweet and tender..."

And there was that. Such a slow, loving, emotional kiss that was, well, not the kind I needed to turn my hips from...

No, this was the kind where I wanted to find somewhere for us to lay down and hold each other.

I wanted her to let it out, not to be afraid of that. Note to self that we were still off the record here...

"Ma'am, let us please go to the couch and lay down together. My knees aren't going to last very long with us standing here on my favorite anti-fatigue pad..."

I put my hand out, and she immediately grabbed it. I led the way to the couch, getting situated like I was the other night.

It was just so important for us to share the emotions, the experience, and the energy together. It was part of the core of who Punis and Jessica were, are, and will be. It's what made us, us.

"Ma'am, thank you for sharing with me and giving me insight into your feelings. I appreciate that more than you could know."

"Sir, and I love you irregardlessly."

P36 - or LS-Knee?

Part 36 thirty-six of The Jessica Files. This week, we learn how LSE and my knee suffer a twist of fate.

LSE was going to be doing a moderately not unacceptable concert on 4/20, of course, and Jessica knew as soon as it was posted on their site, lowselfesteem.rocks. LSE was a big part of our lives for a very long time.

"Sir, I request off the record."

I stared at this most excellent human, my life partner. "Jessica, I grant you off the record."

"Sir, as you know, LSE is going to be playing on 4/20/20 at 4:20 pm, Sir. I would like to see LSE, and I know you will, too. I'm asking for your thoughts, Sir.

"Sir, can we? Please, Sir? It'd be us, totally us."

And I cut her off. "Ma'am, you are memorable, and I would like us to experience them live together again.

"Jessica, I will make the arrangements. This show will be live with no crowd. That's so LSE."

"Sir, that's so them, Sir."

Hmm, I can't recall the last time that Jessica was so anticipatory about something. But then, I recalled the last time was to see Greenland Floyd when we first started dating, before **P10 ten Collars**.

"Sir, can I please go back on the record now?"

I gave her a customary head nod, and got back to it.

"Ma'am, I will ensure that we can watch them live, on Pay Per View, only, and if only, you can give me a sweet and tender..."

POW! Right on, my kisser. We fell on the couch. That's how strongly Jessica pounced on me. I was shocked. I err uhh fuck what? How where it what am who? I feel like I sound like Q-Bert.

I collected myself from what? Where the fuck am I? Damn, that bitch just dunked on this shit. Fuck, where AM you???

"Jessica! Now that was a kiss to..."

Boom, another massive shot. I could have left this world on that kiss. So immensely loving, caring, tender. It was, hmm, who?

"Jessica, I will ensure we get to see LSE. Even without you, I'd spend any amount of money on seeing them live. I mean to say, I know them.

"You know this to be true. Remember when you met the brothers Marvalious and Arturius for the first time? We were out to dinner at Hello Shen Go, and they came over before ..."

Jessica made an unexpected screeching noise, something you'd expect from a teenager, not a grown-ass adult.

I wanted to reach out and give her ass some digits, as per the contract, but I knew that this wasn't the time. But yes, her ass was going to (laughing to myself) pay for it.

"Jessica, get a hold of yourself!"

"Yes, Sir, I'm sorry, Sir. They are just so..."

"Ahem!"

"I'm sorry, Sir, I mean no disrespect. They are so us, and we are us and..."

"Jessica, if you want to continue this conversation, you need to be off the record. You know this to be true."

"I'm so sorry, Sir. I mean no disrespect. Please, Sir, know that I'd never! Not with them, Sir!"

"Jessica, kneel before me!"

I sat back on the couch, my shit-ass right knee not so happy with the angle we had turned it. I felt that one, that one was not good.

The kind of not good like a proctology exam from Captain Hook. I mean, come on now, great goto joke.

I'm thankful that I wear shorts because I could feel that one starting to blow up, the pain moving from a bone on bone to a bone on bone without cartilage.

If you were to ask me at any other time, fuck! Ask me when this happened, and I was still trying to figure out my name. She brought it to the hole, strong style, totally strong style.

But I sat there, not saying a word or leading on to what I knew was the outcome: yet another knee surgery. I'd not been wrong in the past.

This day would be no different.

"Jessica, please..."

"I'm sorry, Sir. I'm so sorry. I didn't mean to."

And I cut her off.

"Ma'am, shut the fuck up, ok?"

Wow, that was strong and terse, not something I'd denote from me. But I could feel my right knee going into business for itself. BLEEP!

"I need you to go get me a gel ice pack, the L15, plus the standard dressage I would need. I believe I misstepped and tweaked it.

"I also need you to get me two Dr. Good Knee's Pain-b-gones in 500 mg. Please and thank you."

"Sir, yes Sir. I will do that for you. I love you, Sir."

And off she went to fulfill the request.

Wow, who the fuck am I? I'm all over the map right now. I need to get my shit together because there is no positive outcome.

But this guy knows the score. I could not place blame here, not on Jessica. If I were to do so, there are rules and guidelines to this. I'd have to...

I did not want to be subject to a full inquiry. I was not going all that. Mother fuckers gonna need to saw my shit-ass BLEEP ass knees off. I'm before I allow anyone...

No, no one. I loved my Jessica way too much for that. I will never, ever let anyone come between us again. Fool me once. Shame on eXXa. That's right, and I'll detail that more in another chapter, but that bitch was the poison.

I trailed off a little, knowing that I would kill all humans for her. I'd kill all humans with her. She was that one, my one, the only one.

Wow, I was really up there in my mind. The pain was starting to become excruciating.

Jebus, what the fuck is going on with me? I'm all over the goddamn map. Between that kiss, the twist, the pain...

And to boot, this guy is being spicy all over that bitch. Pain will do that to you.

"Jessica, LSE plays in two weeks. It happens to be a Tuesday. How do you feel about taking the day off?"

"Sir, what a wonderful idea. Is the show at 4:20, as per norm?"

"Yes, ma'am, they shouldn't be allowed to play otherwise." Strong shit from this guy with the softball-sized knee.

I could feel the swelling and pain coming back around for me. It was like a pain boomerang. Hmm, maybe that'll be the title of one of my upcoming books.

This has all the signs of the beginning of a not-so-good part of my life.

But I did have her. This was not a good spot for me, and I could feel the pain coming as I put my leg up on the couch before trying to recline as much as possible.

I knew... I knew what it was...

"Sir, this is all my fault. Please forgive me and let me service you however I can..."

"Jessica, please stop..." I paused. "Please come here and kneel before me."

"Before Zod?" Jessica added.

"Ma'am, might I remind you of your station? Your role? Ma'am, that was highly disrespectful. How dare you."

I started to giggle and then chuckle. "Bitch, present yourself to me,now!"

And boom, there she was. My one.

"Jessica, I love you. There could be no doubt. I am, however, in a lot of pain, and I surely could use the ice pack and the aspirin I asked for. Like 5 minutes ago, which is when I asked for it."

I could see the onset of panic in Jessica's eyes. She's about as much off of her game tonight as I am. We are both all sixes and sevens.

Jebus, that kiss... What a destroyer. Hmm, what another wonderful idea for a book title. That's weird.

And then there was Jessica, all of the gear in tow. She handed me a small glass of water and two pills; they could have been quaaludes for all I knew, and I did not care so long as they helped with the pain.

"Jessica, there are two additional requests that I must ask of you based on recent events. Or how my knee just got jacked up again."

"I need a medium pillow from the hall closet, you know the one, so I can elevate my knee to help with the swelling.

"But, Ma'am, I have another request. And I'm sure you'll question it, but I do not care. I need a triple and some Sour Zed. Absolutely now.

"I love you, Jessica. There could be no doubt. For this lifetime and the next, you are mine as I am yours. I really, really do love you, and I know that every bit inside of you knows this to be true.

"OK, I'll shut the fuck up. The request, pretty please." Like I needed to do that. She was required to fulfill my request within the guidelines of the law and the contract. Note the order, like usual.

Man, the pain was blowing up right now. I should have asked for a Scarface-sized tray of cocaine while I was at it. Or, for us to go see Annie Stezia. She's myyyyyy... and I trailed off in my mind, thinking about that spot.

Boom, there was Jessica. "Sir, first and foremost, the pillow. I would like to place it under your knee. Is that something you require assistance with?"

At this point, I was done with this shit. "Jessica, for the next 15 minutes, I grant you off the record."

I tapped and moved about on my watch, totally not setting the timer for 15 minutes.

"Punis, I'm so sorry. This is all my fault. I shouldn't ha..."

"Bitch, enough. I love you. There is no fault here. I mean, except it is your fault." I winked at her and busted out laughing. She knew I was being spicy.

"Jessica, this is not your fault. I own this, and that's enough of that. Capisce?"

"Yes, Punis, but I'm worried that..."

"Ma'am, I'll pull my leg up for you to put the pillow in, and we'll adjust accordingly. I will also need a refill on this drink in about 30 seconds. Also, thank you for the delivery, you... wait for this."

I destroyed my sixer of Cromulent Vodka and followed that with a moderate-sized Sour Zed shot. Oh, how that shit hit the spot.

"Jessica, please come sit here next to me before I send you for another errand."

Wow, there's that please word again.

Jessica cautiously sits next to me on the couch as if I'm going to throw her into some wrestling move. I mean, sure, from time to time, I think about it, but now is not the time that I could pull it off.

She inquires, "Sir?"

"Ma'am, you know I am in considerable pain. I'd like to offer you something special here before I request the next round.

"Jessica, my love, and I mean no joke, and as something that will help me get my mind off what is going on..."

I reach my arm out in gently lay it on her lower thigh, just above her knee. Irony. Not a sexual move, although the next part would conjure that up.

"Ma'am, I'd like to fancy you a quickie while I can. It is important to me. You must know this is not your fault, how much I truly love you, and how even in this state, my love for you is so incredibly strong."

I looked at my watch... "Ma'am, you are on the clock."

POW! A sweet and tender, most loving kiss. Not too hard, too soft. Very Goldilocks zone.

"Punis, seriously? I know you are in a tremendous amount of pain and..."

"Jessica, you are on the clock. This is my offer right here and right." POW! Another sweet and tender kiss. I didn't feel off-kilter, I felt...

"Jessica, a quickie doesn't have to be sexual. You could just lay here with me, next to me as you are, as my Jessica."

"Sir? I could!!!"

And in a jiffy, she helped me move over so she could little spoon on the couch. Or so I thought.å No, she lay up against me, her head on my thorax, just like the other night in the tub. It was welcomed and refreshing.

As she lay here with me, holding on to me and resting her head on my thorax, ever so sweetly and lovingly. I took a deep breath. That deep breath. Man, those totally were quaaludes.

"Jessica, I love you, and I'm glad you are lying here with me." As I said that, I pulled the throw blanket from behind me off the back of the couch, and I threw it out towards her, trying not to hit her in the head.

I noticed she didn't move. Oh crap, I'm in no position to try to disappear her... Pfft, she was out cold with an ever-so-slight snore. It was another feature of Jessica that I came to know and love over the years, how many they are now.

I wasn't giving her a quickie here, no, not at all. She was getting an extended off the record. And an incredibly generous offer.

P37 - or The Game?

Part 37 thirty-seven of The Jessica Files. This week, we learn more about why dreams under anesthesia shouldn't be written about.

"Jessica, come on now... It's time to go... we have some most excellent seats to see the Symphony. You damn well know this is important to me."

I paused for what seemed like a million, billion, trillion nano-seconds. Or forever.

"Jessica, are you ready... already?"

"Yes, Sir, I'll be there in one minute. I'm just finishing getting ready so I can accurately represent my feelings to you."

Ahhh fuck. She just blew me up. She just blew up the spot. I mean, she was most excellent without makeup, in sweats... she was too sweet. (Yes, wrestling reference.)

"Ma'am, please?

"Sir, are you dressed appropriately for the Symphony?"

"Ma'am, are you stalling? You damn well know I'm dressed appropriately, as per our dually signed contract. I mean, come on now..."

I chuckled to myself. I'd gone to great lengths to keep my tuxedo in tip-top shape, even having brought it into the dry cleaners last week in anticipation of this most monumental occasion.

Sometimes I wonder if Jessica knew the lengths I'd go to, and then... boom...

Jessica walks into the room. A fucking showstopper. And traffic stopper. A heart stopper. I just looked at her, mouth open, staring at this most impressive human. Fuck!

"Sir? Are you here with me?

"Sir, you look so handsome that I'm going to come over there, kiss you like a fool, hug you like you were none other..." and Jessica trailed off for a second.

"Fuck, I'm sorry, Sir. I think I may have lost my brain here. You are just so handsome. I can't believe I can call you mine as you can call me yours.

"Sir, holy fucking shit, you are really breathtaking!!!"

I stood there wondering where the fuck was she that she was so blown away? Was she thinking about Lexie Blue and Foxy Monroe? Or... or super fucking high?

I trailed off in my mind, thinking about... Just so we are clear here... And I trailed off again. Fuck.

"Jessica, thank you for the compliment. That is so kind, loving, amazing of you. So super ultra mega shiny of you. Damn!!!"

Jessica walked towards me in what could only be described as an evening gown, perhaps a ballgown. A silver and red sequined gown with one shoulder bare. It was so fitting that the fitment fit her so well.

She was resplendent in her radiance. Shit, I can not get trapped up here in my mind. She was too much.

I walked to her, my arms out, to hug and hold her. She knew I knew, and I knew she knew. A lot of knew, I knew.

"Ma'am, you are breathtaking. Jaw-dropping. The everything. Oh, and your dress is magnificent. You, Ma'am, are eternal.

"Jessica, you are by far the most spectacular human ever in the existence of the human race. You are absolute..."

And Jessica cut me off. "Sir, my Sir. You are so hot that you are making me sweat."

And we both laughed. She was, funnily, being spicy.

"Jessica, are you ready? I think they've warmed up for us. You know, they are playing in Hanger 18." And I winked the wink of all winks.

"Yes, Sir, let's hope there are no trains or tornadoes that would make me sweat bullets."

Holy fucking shit, was she not the most... fuck... I'd lost my brain. She was just so goddamn magnificent.

"Jessica, my love of all loves, there are no trains here to take us to Consequences, New Mexico."

We smiled that smile, the one of "one-ups manship."

"Sir, we both know there's a Punishment Due if we don't..."

"Jessica, my love of all loves, you are Polaris."
And there was that pause, the pause where we looked into one another's eyes and said, "Bitch, this shit is on!"

"Jessica... name your game because I will nuke the planet, Polaris style."

"Sir, are you being a supervillain?"

I smiled that sideways smile, knowing it was now on! "Bitch, name your game..." and I laughed hard.

"Fine, Sir. The topic is kinda **Overkill**. I'll start. If you feel the fire, it's because we are taking over."

"Ma'am, are we rotten to the core?"

Jessica snarled at me, having lost round 1. I could see her thinking.

"Sir, well played. I hope you know I'm not under the..."

"Jessica, we'd live in a mad gone world for us to never say never before the end of the line."

"Sir, another well-played round. You are going to own me here, aren't you?"

I gestured to Jessica to bring it. You know, like the Rock would... oh man, maybe too much of the wrestling of late...

"OK, Sir, I'm going to bring it. Strong style... If I were Frankenstein, I'd be reading my horrorscope having just come out of a coma in the new machine.

They'll say that you live young, die free, and I'll say it's a nice day for a funeral."

"Jessica!!!! That's five stars. That was most impressive. Most amazing. Like a real skull crusher."

I paused. This time, it was that pause... "Jessica, it lives. Else, we're F.U.C.T., and I'm half past dead. Nothing is going to save me from the promises I've made, I'm all right, though. BUT...

This is my December, and my revelation is that the stone-cold Jesus, the one with the forked tongue, made me understand that I am fear, 80 cycles around, and running that black line."

Boom! Mic dropped by this guy. No overcoming that one. She'd brought it to the hole, and I smacked that shit straight down.

"Bitch, I love you far too much not to accurately represent myself in this game. You know you can never win, right? That's why I love you. Jess....sica."

I grinned at her. If she wanted it to be "on," this shit was gonna be "on." I'd immediately bury her ass within the constructs of the contract. She was stunned, totally stunned by the dramatic turn of events. Dunking on her, mucho supremo.

"Sir, you are super ultra mega hot. And after the symphony, I'm going to attack you within the rules and guidelines of the contract."

I put my hand out to Jessica and stated. "Ma'am, let us go to our seats."

We walked to the couch, Jessica sat (you know because it's our fucking couch), and I sat myself down.

"Jessica, my love, do you Trust me?" And I winked at her. The game was still on, and we both knew it. I wanted her to dunk on this shit, end it so I could smile lovely at her knowing she was "her."

"Sir. I love you... I heard that Lucretia was angry again because she couldn't remember what all of the five magics were, but then in her darkest hour... she...she..."

Jessica was stumbling. It was cute.

"Sir, she... shit! I'm sorry, Sir. You were right, I can never win."

"Jessica, it's OK. I love you anyways. Now then, are we ready for the show?"

"Yes, Sir. You can hit play now."

I smiled that smile. The crazy shit we do in the name of love and the contract.

"Ma'am, here we go. It's August 20th, 2021. The first dance." And I laughed like a supervillain. More wrestling references.

"Godzilla 2014. Blu-ray. Master Audio 7.2. No subtitles. Just the king... The king is back, baby." Once again, wrestling reference. Man, we need to pull this shit back a little.

"Sir, I know this is your favorite movie aside from The Naked Gun. I'm so glad that I can be here with you to share the experience together. It means the world to me."

I turned to my left, where she would always be for this lifetime and the next. I smiled. "Jessica, you are so everything. I love it when we play this game. I love listening to you. You are just... you really are phenomenal, Jessica."

I paused; this time, it was the pause of "Do I want to watch the movie or be mauled by the... fuck, brainfade... #winning lol"

"Jessica, I'm only kidding about watching Godzilla tonight. There's only one movie that is worthy of your time, something that takes us back... way back..."

"But remember, Ma'am, plants crave it." And there it was, another mic drop. This guy. And I smiled that smile of a million, billion, trillion smiles.

"This is why I love you more, Sir. Idiocracy for the mother fucking win!!!"

P38 - or Pain?

Part 38 thirty-eight of The Jessica Files. This week, we learn more about Pain. Yeah, that's about all of it.

I sat there on the couch, my BLEEP ass knee elevated, gel ice pack in tow, and nicely wrapped up. A joyless setup, the pain kicking me in the junk over and over...

Yeah, that shit. That relentlessness, perhaps repentlessly (a Puniverse word), of what I was dealing with. But... I did have someone spectacular in my life.

I had her. The one. The bringer of light. The one to make me complete. She was completed. Absolute 0, like time itself. She was all. Everything. Magnificence.

That was Jessica. Endless. That one, that friend who was there for you for so long. You loved them if not for only the fact that they showed you what the love of a friend was. Someone who knew what it meant to be a real friend. Absolute, like time itself.

Jessica had explained it in the past to me; she was just so spectacular.

But that's not the subject of this topic. No, it's much less important. Perhaps impressive? Or...

Jessica walked into the room. It's like traffic stopped. I mean, at least in the room, it did. The cats just sat still. I surely did, too; I mean...

"Sir, are you OK? Is there something that I can do for you?"

"Jessica?"

"Sir, I love you. There could be no doubt. But I'm here to take care of you post-surgery. Hell, for life..." And being the most adorable and amazing human to have ever been a human and lived in and among us, she dropped a "For Life," NWO style.

I think we've watched too much wrestling. Or, we were both dorks who loved wrestling.

Jessica would tell me, from time to time, about growing up watching AWA/NWA Wrestling with her father, whereas I grew up watching WWF. So many entertaining wrestlers, hot damn. But we had wrestling as another thing to bind us together. But as you've seen and you will see, lots of spots that relate to wrestling relate to our lives.

I mean to say, I wasn't worried about her going to the top ropes and dropping an elbow on me, Randy "Macho Man" Savage style. Boy, howdy, how that move, growing up, inspired and spoke to me.

I'd..., and I trailed off. "Jessica, my love. My love of all loves... I love you, Ma'am. There could be no doubt. Thank you for being here to help me."

"But, Sir, it's my pleasure and honor."

Another time where the contract blows us up. No, not in a bad way. It's just... sometimes the lengths we go to in the contract... It's just so...

I loved her, and there could be no doubt. And she loves me, and there could be no doubt. Absolute in our love... I was way the fuck up there, wasn't I now?

I mean, I'd not taken any painkillers post-surgery; that's not my style. I'm more of a one-bill, Phil, kinda guy... but I had her. I had her to help and take care of me; such a super fucking star was she. Billy Graham style.

"Jessica, my love, would you get me a refill of my V/Z? Please?" Damn, it's not like I needed to add the please, but god damn, she meant the world to me, and the level of love and respect I tried to show her...

Wow, way up there still. I know my mind was trying to block the pain, and I feel we often resort to more animalistic or primitive forms of our personalities. No, this wasn't an excuse to be a dick.

This was... fuck, still way up there. Where the fuck was my drink?

"Jessica, my dear... I ordered 177.4412 ccs of liquid pain-be-gone, as Dr. Goodknee suggested. I mean, come on now, for fuck's sake."

And I hear Jessica say, "Thank you, Dr. Goodknee, for checking in on us. He's a little cranky, but, well, you've met him..." And she giggled.

Normally, I'd have owned her for that, but I love her way too much... Sometimes, what the DORCs don't know... now that's a fucking recipe for destruction. Man, I'm so up there I'm hearing a Symphony.

"Jessica, second call before I get up, walk to the kitchen, and pour myself my own FUCKING drink!"

That was totally for effect, and I wasn't going anywhere. This shit hurt like a mother fucker, up and down, coast to coast, not even a boomerang. Just pain. You know, sometimes I loved being up there...

"Sir, I just finished making it, Sir. I'm on my way, Sir. I'll explain..."

"Bitch! Vodka... how dare you???" And I busted out laughing, fully knowing I'd overheard her on the phone. Plus, I loved the fuck out of this human. She was just so shiny, so magnificent.

Jessica arrives with my... umm,... rather very oversized drink, complete with an old-school silly straw. I just looked at her like I was going to throttle her.

And she knew I'd NEVER, evah, allow any harm to come to her that wasn't a line item signed in our contract.

This guy thinks a lot. And this isn't something new

"Sir, I'm sorry. All of our usual hardware is in the dishwasher. We forgot to run it before going to your appointment. I'm sorry, Sir, I mean no..."

"Ma'am, pause, please. It's my responsibility, dually signed in our contract. I should have run it, and I forgot to in the rush to get out this morning. I will report my mistake to the DORCs in the morning."

"Sir, there's no need. I've already covered us with the DORCs. They understood the situation because we told them well beforehand, and as we both know, they appreciate the fuck out of that.

"Sir, I've also gotten us a doctor's note if we need one. That's why I was on the phone, talking with Dr. Goodknee himself. You know he's a HUGE fan of your work, as I reminded him you were of his."

nd that brought a pretty smile from my pretty gal. She was so remarkable, just so shiny. Wait, is that the second time I've noted that? Fuck!

"Jessica, I appreciate your due diligence. That is another reason I love you anyways. You are so much, Jessica... see, I said Jessica and not that name you don't like, Ma'am." Jessica sneered at me, which gave way to a super cute grin.

I know how she felt about me calling her Jess. It's how I felt about being called Dude. But it hadn't happened since our collar ceremony, as best I can recall.

I can only imagine her saying "Dude" over and over and over in response. But I knew she'd never say that to me if not for a slip or by permission. Again, with The Book of LSE references.

I turned to my left, where she'd be for this life and the next, and whispered into her ear, "I grant you off the record, Jess."

I looked at Jessica, and she smiled that smile before extending the silly straw toward me. I mean, what am I seven? Ok, I'm totally not.

I grabbed the mug and straw, and in one fell swoop, I killed that drink. All 177.4412 cc's of liquid pain be gone.

"Jessica, my love. I don't need a fucking straw to..." and POW! Right on my kisser. It was like the one she gave me this morning before surgery. Not that I'm worried about losing you one, just the one where you knew that you had something to come back to.

Jessica was the balance to The Outcome (**P29 - or The Outcome?**). She was the one who put up, whereas the others were all posers, not able to walk the walk.

"Ma'am, I'll take a dozen of those, please. That was rather spectacular. Like you, my love of all loves."

And then Jessica rained down twelve amazingly beautiful kisses, each with more love than the last. She was bringing it to the hole strong, strong style. She was dunking here.

After a moment to collect myself, I turned and stared at Jessica. It was that stare, the one where you knew you were so fucking in love with them that they suddenly realized just how powerful that was and how much you meant to them.

She was that one, the one, my one, there'd be none other. And no spoilers here, but there's a time or two that Jessica emoted the same. She was so shiny.

Fuck, was that the third time?

"Ma'am, have you spoken with the Reverend CD?"

"Yes, Sir. He sent all of his love and wanted me to tell you, when you were up for it, that you were his most excellent friend. He was glad he had me to help you, knowing how much it meant to you when he helped you after surgery #2 on your left knee."

I smiled. If there was someone I loved more than anyone else aside from Jessica, it was the Reverend CD. He was shiny to me, too. Yes, I know I did it once again, the fourth time.

"Ma'am, you let CD know we were all good and provided him updates as he'd expect without asking for them, right?"

"Yes, Sir, as I did with Good Sister, Bad Sister, Dr. Jasmin, Dr. G, Dana, Fry, Mrs B, Kirk..."

"Oh, how I love all of my friends, Jessica. Thank you for updating them all. I know it's a good amount of work... oh, did you talk to my boss as well?"

"Sir?"

"Jessica? I have a boss, right? Am I slipping into a lucid session here?"

"No, Sir, it's just that... well, you own your own business. You own Secret Freezer Publishing. Did you forget?"

"No, Jessica, I did not forget. I mean to say, did you tell my boss... All of them?" Jessica smiled that smile, the smile of a million, billion, trillion smiles.

"Yes, Sir, I posted on the website and all of our social media accounts." Yes, she said ours. It would always be ours. All of ours. Ours.

P39 - or Cherry Pie?

Part 39 thirty-nine of The Jessica Files. This week, we learn more about April in Phoenix.

I stood there on my favorite anti-fatigue pad. I needed to have an open and honest conversation with Jessica about something very deep. Something very important to me.

"Jessica, present yourself. Now."

And in a jiffy, there she was. The most beautiful, wonderful, and spectacular human quickly walked into the room.

"Here I am, Sir. What do you need?"

"Ma'am, are you here for me, or are you here for yourself?"

"Sir, what does that mean? I don't understand."

"Are you here for me and to be my friend, or are you here for yourself because you're lonely?

"My question to you is, are you missing something in your life and trying to fill it with me, or do you want me in your life to fulfill it?

"I have been in this place, and I have been with those feelings, and I can tell you that there is a distinct and unmistakable difference. And I can tell you from my experience that the two intersect very early and fizzle out shortly after that.

"What I'm trying to say to you is this: are you with me or not?

"I've been here before a time to two when someone was rebounding, and I knew it, but I didn't take advantage of the situation because I am a very good person.

"Because of that, one could say that I had prevented myself from succeeding, but the directive was different. I wasn't after pussy. I was after somebody. Perhaps something greater than the sum of the parts.

"Jessica, I want you all in. All in. I want you to be in such a manner that you are mine as I am yours. I need you to understand that I'm not just along for the ride, but I'm here for the whole fucking show.

"I want everything, and if you're incapable of bringing that, then all you need to do is tell me. I don't mind having you in my life as you and such things, but I can't..." and I trailed off.

"Ma'am, I can't be here without you. I can't exist in this reality without you here with me."

"Sir, are you saying?"

"Ma'am, what is it that you think I am saying?"

"Sir, I mean no disrespect. I'm just not sure I understand what you're saying to me. Please help me understand your feelings so we can bridge this gap.

"Sir, what is the matter? You know I love you inside and out. You know I love you through and through. You know I'd go MDK on anyone that got between me and you, Sir."

"Jessica, my love. You know my love for you is..."

"Sir, I don't mean to cut you off, but I want you to know that my love for you is absolute, like time itself."

"But, Jessica... time is relative and..."

"Sir, Time is absolute, Sir, not relative. Only the perception of time has any relativity." She unusually paused and stated, "Sir, that is just how much I love you."

I stood there, and I stared at this most magnificent human. She was unlike anybody else that I had ever encountered. The sheer level of her intelligence was far, far beyond everybody except for Dr. Jasmin. But we'll save that conversation for another day.

I continued to look at this most wonderful woman, agaze with darkness and hope. Sometimes, I knew that she had brought the antidote to me. But other times, I couldn't see or feel her. She wasn't there anymore.

"Ma'am, that was so sweet and yet educational. I am blown away. Your statement shows me signs of..."

"Sir, I must emphatically state to you that I am all in. That I love you in such an intense and amazing way... I hope one day to show you just how much I love you."

"Ma'am, are you saying that you love me in such an intense manner?"

"Sir, you know this to be true. I love you with everything I have, everything I have been, and everything I will ever be. You are my Bret Hart."

That was about Bret "The Hitman" Hart, a legendary wrestler with such an "it" factor. And fuck, the best there is, the best there was, and the best there ever will be. Yeah, that guy. And he earned it.

"Ma'am, I... I... I...I don't know what to say. You've totally blown up my spot!"

"Sir, I love you. There will be none other. I am yours as you are mine. I am with you till the end of time and the day after, Sir."

I smiled at Jessica, nearly tearing up. And then she made her way to me. I wasn't sure what to expect, what she was up to. I could only gaze at her, frozen in the moment.

"Ma'am, you are so..."

"Sir, please know I am all in. I've been all in far longer than Christmas Eve day, much, much further than that. Sir, you are everything I've ever wanted in a mate. You are so fantastic that I could only pray to Zeus for you to be mine.

"You mean the world to me, Sir. There'll never, evah be another. I am yours as you, I hope, are mine."

I continued to stare at her, blown away by her depth and charisma. She was extraordinary. She was just so marvelous. I... damn it, dude! Don't let her infect your brain with her... I mean, been there, lost money on it???

And at that moment, I let go of myself to her, unknowingly or not, just as she had done in **P26 - or Pre-Starter?**. She gave me a leap of faith, and I know now that is what I need to do. But.. but...

"Jessica, I am fascinated with this facet of you that is most spectacular. You are most fascinating to me. I..."

"Sir, I would kill all humans for you, and I will kill all humans with you. You are the most wonderful, loving, caring, charismatic, intelligent, and humane person I have ever met or had the pleasure of knowing. You are everything to me, Sir.

"Yes, Sir, I am all in. I am here for you. I want to be the whole fucking show. I..." and she paused momentarily. "Sir, I can only further state that I have loved you since before day one, and you know this to be true."

God damn, she was just so... fuck, she'd made me lose my brain once again.

"Jessica, thank you for answering my question. My feelings for you are... " and I stopped, unsure of what I was saying and the ramifications of it.

"Jessica, I can only hope to show you how much I love you one day."

And then POW! Right on my kisser... and who, what? Where? Turn the hips, dude. Now! Dude, brain, borked, umm... Fuck!

Jessica stepped back as I stood there, a puddle of mush suspended in the air somehow. I opened my eyes to see her, see her. Standing there in such a beautiful dress. The kind you would wear for something special.

"Sir, are you OK?"

"Yes, ma'am. That was some kiss, Jessica. I lost my brain there for a moment. Jebus!"

"Sir, let's go. The Reverend CD is patiently waiting for us outside. How many days do we get like this in April? And especially today, the 20th..." And Jessica winked.

I could only smile at that point, so unsure if I could keep it together for her, for me, and for the Reverend CD.

"Sir, if you take my hand, we can let go of ourselves together. We can pledge ourselves to one another, and we can start a new life together."

And I put my hand out to her, smiling all the way. "You passed the test, **Jess**."

ACKNOWLEDGEMENTS

The **Reverend CD** - You are the one constant in my life, my most excellent friend. I write this after I've nearly had my own Chernobyl-level meltdown when I hadn't spoken to you in a couple of days.

You could hear it in my voice when we spoke on the phone. So could your wife, as I was freaking the fuck out.

To anyone who reads this, yes, the **Reverend CD** is the only person I have spoken with daily over the last 6+ years and is still the only reason I bother to write, especially when I feel like there's no point.

Aside from apathy, sir, you are so important to me as a human and have had such a tremendous impact on my life. You've given me ideas, thoughts, pointers, adjustments, suggestions, and on and on. You, sir, are just so important to me as a human that I do not believe I can articulate that in the totality of my life, past, present, and future.

Dr. Jasmin - You continue to be a major player in my life in so many incredible ways. Please know that I am writing this part after we went to dinner, and I <u>specifically</u> told you that the event made me feel like an adult. Only you could do that, **Dr. Jasmin**

You are a great friend who knows so much about me and with whom I have so many loving and fantastic memories.

And who would I be if I left out something far beyond horrific, and you came to console me because of my fucking BLEEP ass knees.

We slept that night as best as we could, given the pain, shuddering, the scariness of having to bear witness to it.

But we slept that night together as two humans, hand in hand, as only the most amazing of friends could do.

And for those who read this, yes, we did sleep together that night, hand in hand, not letting go, regenerating one another's energy, and bringing me back as a human.

That night showed me so much about myself, about you, and about our friendship that I'd be remiss not to include it in this story.

I owe you so much, **Dr. Jasmin** - Thank you for sharing time with me while we've been getting to know each other once again as the humans we are, and helping me fit in.

You really are astonishing. And my love for you is stronger.

———————————————————————

Good Sister - I will only ever have two sisters.

I know that when you come to see me... fuck my BLEEP ass knees! Thank you for showing me the path to redemption and always being positive, encouraging me to do the same.

We've all got our shit, and I learned how to own it from you. Thank you for that, amongst the millions of other things a big sister would do for her little brother.

I love you, **Good Sister**, as I do **Bad Sister**. The three of us are the exception to our parents and their madness. Some of us know this more than others... ahem, **Bad Sister**... 🙂

I love you, **Good Sister**, for being a force of reason throughout my life. You've always been loving, kind, and spectacular. That is what we were taught by those no talent ass clowns.

But wait, there's more as you once again have saved me, saved the boys. I write this with tears in my eyes, knowing just how instrumental you have been in my life.

I owe all that I have in my life to you, **Good Sister**. I mean that with the most sincerest emotions possible. Sho level emotions. Without you, I would not have survived long enough to be trapped on The Other Side, let alone this time and date.

Good Sister, I will only ever have two sisters.

Bad Sister - I will only ever have two sisters.

Bad Sister, you've never done me wrong. EVER. And I remember that email asking me why you were a "BAD" sister.

And I know I chuckled a bunch when I emailed you back.

Bad Sister, you've been detached from my life, as I have from yours, your families. But I know that you love me as only a middle older sister could do. You are, unknowingly, such an incredible force in my life.

No, it's not because you are clearly provably crazier than I am. No, it's more than that. It's that you are one of three, and there'll be none other.

I know you took care of me as a child for ever so long. Through the sicknesses, hospitalizations, and surgeries, all before I was ten years old. You always made sure to take care of me.

I cannot do justice to my perception of your love for me above and beyond your taking care of me. Time and again, you, **Bad Sister**, took care of me.

Where the fuck would I be without you? Oh, I know... I'd never made it there.

I love you, **Bad Sister**. And I will only ever have two sisters.

The Great Daniel L - Sometimes, it's hard to articulate your feelings about another person when it comes to the emotional toll that one pays with another.

You know the toll. You know the physical pain I am in. And yet, you continue to be a rockstar who listens to these stories, one chapter at a time, one month at a time.

One of the reasons I enjoy seeing you is to tell you the latest, knowing that, at some level, you are happy for me and very proud of my turning the pain that I have inside of me into something less worse.

More than all the others here, I wish I'd listened to you. Time and again, I wish I had listened to you. It is perhaps one of the biggest mistakes I've ever made in my life, and perhaps I wouldn't be trapped here.

Fry - I miss you, my friend.

I really could use the phenomenal amount of power that you had and would give to me. But I understand.

You were with me, there on The Other Side. Reading about it, well... I wish you could, but I know I'd never be able to in your position.

I do greatly miss you being a such an important part of my life. You've had a tremendous amount of impact on me, and you know that it'd take a bit to spell all of it out.

Sure, the 1 a.m. phone calls, some years ago, sucked and were shitty of a friend who clearly is a moron, completely incapable of caring for themselves.

And yet, you cared for me and about me for so long. Sometimes, I could listen, and in others...

I really do miss you, my friend.

Mrs. B -You've been there for me to the point where, as a human, today, when I'm writing this, is Saint Kane's day. And when we chatted, you'd have had a shit-tac-ular day. IIRC, your watch said 96% stress levels.

But I didn't say anything because... I knew.

I mean, you know I love your husband, dog, oh, and you, in such a way that I wanted you in my life. And many years ago, you asked about being friends. I jumped on that shit.

No, fuck you, anyone who thinks otherwise. Already had former co-workers who were NTACs. They don't get free copies, bitches.

Mrs. B, you are the one that called me that night. Only you. And while my friends were loving and supportive, you are spectacular.

Dr. G - Thank you for everything you continue to do for me as a human, continuing to transform me into a less screwed-up version of me. See, I didn't say fucked up.

I do enjoy chatting about these stories, the wacky ideas I come up with, and how, from time to time, they make sense on a grander scale.

I feel as if, since I started this train wreck in March of '22, you've heard more about my ideas than any other person and likely all parties combined, including the Reverend CD.

Thank you, **Dr. G.**, for your generosity and love and for showing me the level of care you can give another person. Without you, I'd be far more broken and destroyed in life.

Kirk -We've known one another for 20+ years now, and not until I wrote this, I never thought I'd call you **Kirk** anywhere and at any time outside of the bedroom. Evah, again...

And yet, aside from the ridiculousness of calling you **Kirk** and my love for you as a friend, you've always been you—a friend and a balance.

I know that I'm a pain in the ass, ask Larry, and that my dedication is incredibly deep; also, see Larry. I hope one day he lands here (after learning how to read).

While, as humans, we don't always align, I listen to your thoughts and beliefs, and I have acted upon them repeatedly.

I should have listened about getting married... 😉😂 j/k, she's a good human, and I mean no disrespect to her. But "ex-wife/husband" jokes, man, they write themselves.

Dana -I've told you, privately and in print, just how important you are and will always be to this story. Without you, none of this would have happened. You know this to be true.

I hope one day to show the world just how true the story is, how true our friendship is, and just how much fun it was. And when I do, you will be the first to know.

You are one of the smartest, most loving, honorable, and most fantastic humans I've ever known. There's a reason that you and the **Reverend CD** are in the spots you are.

It's not FLA. No, it's more spectacular than that. You see, without the both of you, none of this happens. I specifically am stating the <u>two of you</u>. Both of you are the most important people to this story, to my life during that time and onwards.

To open and close the most heartfelt acknowledgments I can give, you both kept me alive, moving forwards or at least sideways.

Dana, I really do listen to the voicemail from time to time. The sincerity within and a friend's love towards another can be heard. It is the exceptionalism of who you are and why I will always love you as my friend.

Once again, **Dana**, thank you for helping me try to get over the goal line in this story, all **145,262** lines of it. Yeah, that's the number of lines in our chat history. All of it between friends.

I wish I would have listened better and not ended up...

Oh, and would it kill ya to do another cookie massacre silliness for Festivus this year? 🤗

And lastly... **Sapphire** -**Hey**! I shopped there because of you! And now I'm trapped at the DMV. HELP!

After all, this is a love story in absolute, like time itself.

PXX - or A Special Draft?

Pxx x x of The Jessica Files. This week, we get a small unedited draft of something Punis has been working on, which is only available in the hardcover printing.

"Jessica, like you pulled me back, you gave me a second chance in life and with you. I have to tell you something: it is very important and could be rather shocking.

"When I came back from the DMV, I knew everything. Everything that would happen up until that date and time with us. I just knew. I knew how special and amazing you were. You are just everything. The ultimate partner.

"It is why I said to you, as specifically noted in **P27 - Or Pre-starter?** from **Tales From The Jessica Files - From Bad To Worser**, the following statement, word for word.

"Jessica, get your shit together. I can't exist in this reality without you here with me."

Yes, Sir, I remember that, Sir. I think I am starting to understand."

“What I knew of our life together quickly dissipated from my mind, but the truth was always there. I knew how powerful your soul was to me, and it is a large part of the man who stands in front of you."

"Sir, I am not sure what to say to this dramatic tur... Oh wait, I’m off the record. Punis, I love you, and I feel like I have always known you were too good to be true. And then this series of events.

"I now know why I thought you were too good to be true, Punis. It’s because you’ve gone to hell and come back for me. Your second chance was mine, too. Punis. It was mine, too."

"Jessica, I’m sorry that I’d never told you this. I loved you far too much to let you walk away again. I knew it inside and out then, as I know this to be true even still."

"I love you, Punis. I love you, my Sir. My one and only Sir. You have given me a life that I never thought I would have. You have saved me many times.

Jessica approached me, arms out for a hug. And one she would get.

www.ingramcontent.com/pod-product-compliance
Lightning Source LLC
Chambersburg PA
CBHW020325030826
48979CB00020B/90
9798989468027